The Dre Merchants

and other fantasies

By
Steven J. Scott

MAPLE
PUBLISHERS

The Dream Merchants and other fantasies

Author: Steven J. Scott

Copyright © Steven J. Scott (2023)

The right of Steven J. Scott to be identified as author of this work has been asserted by the author in accordance with section 77 and 78 of the Copyright, Designs and Patents Act 1988.

First Published in 2023

ISBN 978-1-83538-080-2 (Paperback)
     978-1-83538-081-9 (E-Book)

Book Cover Design, Illustrations and Layout by:
     White Magic Studios
     www.whitemagicstudios.co.uk

Published by:
     Maple Publishers
     Fairbourne Drive, Atterbury,
     Milton Keynes,
     MK10 9RG, UK
     www.maplepublishers.com

Contents

Volume 1
Short Stories

The Dream Merchants
Part 1: The Castle of Rainbows

Long before dawn the dreams had tormented him. Each night they were more vivid, more intense. In his mind he saw again the river valley, the high-peaked mountains, the distant castle, and the rainbow skies. He saw again the beautiful maiden, and heard her voice, calling out to him, imploring him to answer, but somehow – try as he might – he could never reach her. His eyes flickered open in the dark, and he tried to calm himself by lying still until his heart stopped thumping. He sat on the edge of the bed and tried to pour himself some water, but his hand was shaking too much to hold the glass. The headache, which never left him, intensified, and a bolt of pain shot through his nerves. As daylight broke, the Emperor Fu bowed his head, and wept.

Six moons had passed since the Emperor had sent his finest and most experienced knights out to scour the land and find the mysterious castle, but all had returned shaking their heads and downcast. Now, finally, he decided it was time to seek help, and so, disguising himself as an elderly fisherman, he made his way towards the harbour.

The Emperor sat for a long time watching the boats. The fishing fleet had just returned, and junks, skiffs and cargo vessels jostled for space along the quayside. The entire harbour was a hive of activity as men and women worked together, hauling goods to and fro, unpacking crates, loading the catches, and all the time singing and laughing as they rushed to get the work done before sundown.

Many times, he had visited this place as a child, quietly sitting with his father for hours, watching the mariners, tradesmen, ship-owners and merchants. All were part of this community bound together by the one thing they had in common – the sea.

The Emperor often thought of his father these days. He had been a big burly man, imposing, boisterous, and often causing mayhem at court with his over-zealous and outrageous behaviour. Even so, he commanded respect and admiration from all those around him.

It grew late as the Emperor remembered.

Eventually Fu rose and made his way towards a large and busy tavern near the waterfront. The Seafarer's Inn had been standing long before the city of Qan and the docks had been built, and some said, before the sea itself began to lap at the shore. There was indeed a mystical element about the Seafarer's Inn. The sign of the laughing dolphin swung outside the oak-panelled door, and once inside, the inn became a pure treasure-trove for all those whose livelihood was the sea.

The interior was lit by ships' lanterns, and the names of famous and mythical vessels were carved into the wooden floor: the *Pioneer*, the *Golden Phoenix*, the *Spirit of Shadows*, and many others. Two crossed harpoons were fixed against the far wall, along with paintings and etchings of wondrous sea-creatures, from huge whales and monstrous squids to great shoals of tiny plankton which seemed to move and dart as your eyes followed them. The shelves were piled high with books, manuscripts, ships' logs, charts, and sea-lore of every kind.

The Emperor had always loved the Seafarer's Inn. As a young man his father had brought him here to taste his first wine, and to be regaled by the tall tales told by the outlandish proprietor.

Mr. Po had become a legend. His swinging moustaches, fish-scale tattoos, and inevitable fez were part of the folk-lore of the sea. He had been a pirate, soldier, assassin, spy, preacher, wrestler in the Imperial Circus, and finally, the owner of the Seafarer's Inn. He smoked a long thin pipe filled with dubious substances, and wore a flowing robe which appeared to be part of him, never impeding his cat-like movements. His laughing eyes and easy-going manner belied his sharp intelligence – and his uncanny abilities with sword, knife or bow.

Mr. Po had instantly recognised the Emperor, despite his disguise, and his smile beamed with pleasure. The Emperor lowered his hood. "So good to see you again, Mr. Po." They clutched hands. "I would like a glass of your finest wine." He spoke quietly. "I would also like to see the Net-weavers, if they are here?"

"Aye, but I'll take none of your coin." Mr. Po leaned forward and whispered. "They are in the Cabin – they've been in there all week. Sire, you look weary. Trouble? My sword is yours, always." The Emperor placed his hand on Mr. Po's shoulder. "Not that kind of trouble, old friend." He emptied his glass, and glanced across at an unmarked door.

"My lord," Mr. Po kept his voice down. "Be careful."

The Cabin was one of the labyrinth of rooms that made up the Seafarer's Inn. It was a small, circular room where fishing gear, sails, and clothing were repaired. The Emperor hesitated in the doorway. He felt a strong foreboding, and nearly turned away. "Enter." The voice was that of a young woman.

In the centre of the room sat three women who were working on fixing the damaged nets of the fishermen. Two of the women seemed ancient, but their hands were untouched by age, and had lost none of their grace and dexterity. The third woman looked much younger, and was fair of face and figure. "Ladies, may I sit?"

"Sire, you are our guest."

The Emperor smiled. "I knew that I could hide nothing from you."

One of the older women nodded. "We know why you have come, but first, you must make payment." He had been expecting this.

"Very well. I have brought gold."

"Gold is of no use to us."

"Then what ...?"

"If you wish to know your future, there is a price." The younger woman smiled up at him.

The Emperor left knowing no more than when he had arrived. He was aware that no amount of coercion could make the women speak against their will – and the price they had demanded was too high.

As he watched the Emperor slip away into the night, Mr. Po felt uneasy.

"Fate has overtaken us," he murmured, and relit his pipe.

On his return to the palace the Emperor called his counsellors together to tell them he was leaving on a quest to find the rainbow castle. His advisers warned him against making such a perilous journey, for the lands beyond his realm were wild and inhabited by fierce and unworldly creatures. The Emperor, however, knew he had no choice, for he must find the castle, or else be driven mad by these relentless dreams and visions.

And so, on a bleak winter morning, the Emperor and a small band of warriors rode out through the palace gates.

For a year and a day, they searched. They crossed the mighty river Yue, which bordered the kingdom, skirted Talon Forest, and journeyed through the Southern Lands until they reached the Mermaid Straits. Here they crossed into the great Su Desert, where they nearly died of thirst and heat exhaustion. They followed the Pilgrim's Trail north through the desolate Plains of Zuru, and finally traversed the Ice Shallows and wandered the Frozen Lands, with the spectre of the huge Glacier Mountains looming over them.

The Emperor's soldiers were loyal, and fought by his side, but the search seemed fruitless, and their numbers were dwindling. One intensely cold evening, as the men tried to warm themselves around a meagre fire, the Emperor took the Commander, a trusted friend he had known since childhood, to one side and began to speak:

"Commander Chang, I cannot ask you to go any farther. You and your men have been the best and bravest companions I could ever have hoped for, but our quest has been costly, and to no avail. Tomorrow we return home, for I fear we will never find the rainbow castle, and the beautiful maiden – the one I love more than my life – must forever remain but a dream to me."

Chang protested, but the Emperor shook his head, and so, with heavy hearts, they rose early and began the long journey home. However, so far had they travelled, that within an hour's riding they realized that they were completely lost. A storm was gathering, and as the rain became heavier they approached what looked like the remains of a deserted fortress, and rode closer in the hope of finding shelter.

A mighty battle had taken place here. The ground was covered in ashes and the remnants of charred wagons, siege engines and horses. The walls of the fortress, once high and strong, had been breached by some tremendous force, and were now reduced to crumbling ruins. But there was something worse, a deep sense of wrongness, the screams of men … women … children, and the Emperor knew that great evil had been at work here – pain, executions, atrocities.

The Emperor's horse, Xin, a fine white stallion, prodded at the broken ground. Chang drew his sword, and made ready to advance. "No." The Emperor placed his hand on Chang's shoulder. "We'll find somewhere else. Let's leave this place. There are only ghosts here now."

✳

They rode on for the rest of the day, until evening, when the Emperor spotted a small stream, and nearby, a clearing and some fallen logs. "We'll camp here for the night," he said, and as he spoke these words a sudden weariness fell upon him and his followers, and after seeing to the horses they lay down on their blankets to rest.

The Emperor passed a troubled night and got little sleep. Just before dawn he wrapped his cloak around him, and made his way towards a huge rock overlooking a wide river valley. In the distance he could make out a mountain range with light clouds drifting around its highest peaks.

Back at the camp the men were stirring. The Emperor showed them the river valley and mountains. "This is where my dream began," he whispered. "The castle is on the other side of the valley." The soldiers looked confused, thinking that perhaps the Emperor had lost his reason due to his fatigue and sufferings. The Emperor saw this in their faces.

"Do not worry. I know this is the place – I must go on alone." They argued and tried everything to dissuade him, but the Emperor ordered them to stay behind. "Wait for me here. Do not try to follow – you will see me again."

After embracing them all, he rode off alone. The soldiers were crestfallen, but Chang turned to his warriors. "We will do as the Emperor has commanded. But if he does not return within two sunrises, we will go after him."

The Emperor rode on through the valley. It was the most wondrous he had ever seen. Tall trees stood all around, their dew-wet leaves strung together like the most fragile of gossamer webs. The river running through the valley was calm and peaceful, and the Emperor found himself overwhelmed by the ever-changing beauty of this wilderness.

He continued on slowly, feeling the gentle heat of the sun on his face. He felt as a child in a new world which he was becoming part of. He would have given anything not to lose this feeling, for suddenly, the Emperor felt young again.

On the other side of the valley the mountains loomed up as if to touch the sky, and the Emperor was certain that from the summit you could see not only everything of this world, but of all other worlds, for the top of these mountains was surely the home of the gods.

A short while later he spotted the towers of the castle in the distance, and a fading rainbow in the sky, and he knew his journey was coming to an end.

The Emperor approached and slowed his horse. He felt a nervous exhilaration as the enormous castle came into view. The castle's towers were so high he could barely make out the top battlements, and the walls were made of thick stone, ornately covered with clusters of emeralds and pearls.

A wide moat surrounded the castle. The Emperor was wondering how to proceed when a huge drawbridge was slowly lowered. Xin prodded a hoof tentatively at the edge of the drawbridge, reluctant to advance. On looking down the Emperor immediately saw the reason for Xin's hesitation, the bridge appeared to be made of some insubstantial material – one moment it was solid, and the next it seemed almost invisible. As they began to cross, the bridge became more substantial underfoot, and the Emperor could see that the bridge was made from the bones of some gigantic creature. Half way across, he gazed into the waters of the moat, and could see his own image looking back at him. Somehow, he seemed like a stranger, and barely recognized himself.

At the entrance of the castle there were no guards, but two stone unicorns stood either side of a high arched portcullis. He was about to call out to request admittance when the portcullis began to rise, and the Emperor rode through into the castle.

A stable lad appeared, dressed in green, with a heavy towel slung over his shoulder. The Emperor dismounted, and drew some coins from his inner pocket. "Take care of him." The lad nodded solemnly, and led the horse away.

The Emperor entered the courtyard of the castle and gasped in wonder. The courtyard was adorned with crystals and precious stones, and arrayed with flowers and plants of a kind unknown to him. In the centre of the courtyard a plain wooden table stood, and at this table sat the beautiful maiden of the Emperor's dreams.

The maiden wore a gorgeous white dress of shimmering silk, and her beautiful long hair flowed to her waist. She was sitting quietly, lost in thought, and sitting opposite her was the strangest being the Emperor had ever seen. They were both scrutinizing a game that resembled chess. The opposing armies were carved of wood, representing soldiers, squires, holy men, princes, and queens, all protecting a vulnerable king. Each piece rested on a square of dark or light, and the Emperor couldn't help but notice how the board resembled the flagstone squares upon which he was standing.

✳

On seeing the Emperor, the maiden rushed to greet him, and held his face in her hands.

"I knew you would find me. I knew it!"

The Emperor was overcome with joy, and could barely speak.

"I nearly lost hope of ever finding you." They stood together for some time, until the Emperor turned to face the stranger, who had risen from the table, and now stood before them.

"Who ... or what are you?" he asked.

"I have many names – and none, but for our purposes, Kassion will suffice. Some call my race the Dream Merchants, which is as good a name as any." The Emperor bowed, for he could sense that he was in the presence of great power. He also knew instinctively, that this being was not of his world. Kassion motioned for him to be seated. "I welcome you to our castle, Emperor Fu, please help yourself to wine and fruits." Fu seated himself, and began to study the extraordinary and enigmatic stranger.

The Dream Merchant was tall and thin. His pale face was beardless, and he looked both young and old, his eyes deep and unfathomable. He wore a long magician's cloak that seemed to hold every star in the sky, but when he looked closer, the Emperor saw the stars slowly fading, burning out, only to be replaced by other stars, new-born and shining brightly. The cloak was held together by a half-moon amulet of unknown origin.

The Emperor sat down, and the lady poured him a fine colourless wine which had an exquisite taste and lingered on the tongue. The Emperor turned to the Dream Merchant. "The dreams," he asked, "was it you who sent them to me?"

"Ah, dreams. Who really sends them to us? Can we ever be sure? Or perhaps they are ... of our own making? And sometimes, of course, it is possible to exchange one dream ... for another." Kassion rose. "I will leave you for a while." And with that, the Dream Merchant bowed, and slowly turned and left the courtyard.

"I am somewhat confused by his replies," Fu stuttered.

"I wish I could explain ... let us walk together."

As they walked, the Emperor felt he were between waking and dreaming, but he was not afraid any more. "If this is a dream, I would gladly stay here with you." He touched her hair, and kissed her hands. "I know I have always loved you, and yet I do not even know your name."

"I am called Liena, and I cannot remember a time when I have not lived in this castle."

Later the Dream Merchant returned, and for a moment his image appeared distorted, almost ethereal. He seemed to be struggling against some external force, sapping his energy. However, the moment passed, but when he spoke his voice was full of sadness and regret.

"It is time. Liena – it is time."

Liena held his hands, and there were tears in her eyes as she bade farewell to the strange magician. He took a silver pendant from around his neck and placed it around hers.

"Remember me, Liena," he whispered, and then closed his eyes and concentrated. He muttered a long incantation, and slowly two gates began to form at the far end of the courtyard. The first gate was wrought of shining horn, which seemed almost transparent in the sunlight. The second was intricately carved from the ivory of unknown creatures, and embellished with runes and symbols in languages long forgotten. The Dream Merchant spoke softly:

"One gate leads to truth. The other leads into the realm of dream, from which you will never return. But beware, for truth can be deceiving. It is the colour of a rainbow – and dreams – dreams are sometimes real." The Emperor took Liena by the hand.

"You choose."

And she smiled at him, with laughter in her eyes, and led him through the ivory gate.

It was dawn, and a chill was in the air. Chang and his warriors were preparing to begin their search for the Emperor, when one of them noticed something afloat on the lake.

"Look there!" He called to the others.

Chang dismounted, and peered across the water.

"A small boat, heading towards us."

They rushed down to the water's edge as the boat reached the shore. In the boat was the body of the Emperor, laid out respectfully in his imperial colours, a look of profound peace on his face. Chang knelt down beside him, and kissed him once upon the forehead.

"My friend." He spoke hoarsely. "So, you found your dream at last." He turned to the others. "Follow me, I know the way now."

They took his body back with them, and crowds lined the streets amidst great sorrow and mourning, for the Emperor had been kind-hearted, and was much loved by his people.

Part 2: The Siege

"I'm tired of swordplay." The young boy grinned mischievously at his friend. "Let's go into the woods."

"We shouldn't really. We should stay in the courtyard. You know they say the woods are dangerous."

"You aren't frightened, are you?"

"You know I'm not scared. Come on then – I'll race you to the tall oak!"

The two friends climbed over the courtyard gate and scampered off into the woods. They raced through thickets and around huge, broad trees. Finally, they stopped in a large clearing, panting for breath.

"I won!" The younger boy laughed.

"You did not. We got here together."

"Ah, but I've still won – because I've touched the tall oak first." And with that the boy jumped up, and he was just able to reach an overhanging bough of a magnificent oak standing in the centre of the clearing.

The smaller boy punched him lightly on the arm, but then his expression grew serious. "They say the tree has magic, do you think it's true?"

"Maybe. Perhaps … if we both made a wish, we would know. I mean, we would know if the wishes come true."

Solemnly both boys placed their hands on the trunk of the old oak tree, closed their eyes, and made their silent wishes.

The sun was going down, and the woods grew darker. Several times the boys thought they'd heard a strange scuffling noise, and then suddenly a huge sabre-bear with giant tusks and claws was hurtling towards them. "Run! Run! Don't stop!" The smaller boy pushed his friend forward, and turned towards the bear, picking up a nearby rock as a weapon.

The sabre-bear was only a heartbeat away when two arrows took it through the neck, killing it where it stood on top of a boulder, ready to pounce.

The taller boy had stumbled. The other boy stood shaking, and let the rock fall from his hand. A man's voice spoke, and Tung, the Emperor's champion archer, approached. "Chang! You're always in trouble!"

Tung looked sternly at the other boy. "And you, you think you could kill a sabre-bear with a rock?" He knelt down and spoke quietly to the boy. "Fu, one day you will be Emperor – you should know better." He shook his head, but smiled. "Come on, let's get back to the palace – your father will be displeased!"

Chang stirred in his dream, and the scene began to fade from his mind as an insistent knocking brought him back to consciousness. "All right! All right!" He shouted. It was barely dawn, and Chang had hardly slept. He unbolted the door and pushed it open. A uniformed guard saluted and stepped back.

"Commander – we have word that the enemy is moving."

Almost immediately following the sombre funeral of the Emperor Fu, the city of Qan had found itself under siege. Lord Feng, ruler of the eastern kingdom of Zark, had wanted to take Qan intact, and enthrone himself as Emperor of the Southern Lands. Under a flag of truce Feng had demanded the city's complete surrender. From the battlements, Chang had made a short reply: "Not while I'm Commander." And so, Feng's army waited outside the gates, trying to starve the city into surrender.

The banner of the black falcon swirled high above their tents.

Chang sighed. The siege had dragged on from the long humid summer into the bitterly cold winter months. The enemy had made their presence known by lighting torches in the hillsides, unleashing

17

hopeful volleys of arrows every few hours, and maintaining a persistent drumming, often lasting through the night. All this was a deliberate attempt to prey on the nerves of the soldiers and townspeople, and unsettle their leaders. Chang continued to tell himself that these tactics were commonplace, and never worked – he almost convinced himself.

This latest move was obvious. Feng was feigning retreat, deliberately trying to draw Chang's soldiers out. As soon as the gates were open Feng would re-group and attack, and Chang's army would be outnumbered and cut down mercilessly. Chang shook his head and whispered under his breath: "*No, Feng, you'll have to do better than that.*" Aloud he said to the guard. "Where is Captain Yan?"

"In the stables, sir, checking the horses."

Chang found Captain Yan tending to a lively and spirited colt. The Captain was a veteran of many battles, and one of the bravest and best with a sword. Chang returned his salute.

"At ease, Captain. How are the men?"

"They would rather be fighting than waiting, sir, but none of us think they can last much longer out there, not in this weather."

"Captain, they may be getting desperate. They might try something soon. Remember – let nobody in from outside. No spies. No tricks. I want your best men on the gates – at all times!"

"Understood, Commander."

Chang considered his options. The main question on Chang's mind was: for how long could Feng continue the siege? An army in the field needed fresh food and water, or soon morale would slip and mercenaries would start deserting. His own people had enough food stocked up to last through the winter if necessary, but they were unable to send out any fishing boats, as Feng had three warships patrolling the harbour. The situation could not go on forever, but for now all he could do was wait it out … and Chang was not good at waiting.

✳

Lord Feng pulled up his horse and looked back at the city. The gates remained closed. His ploy had not worked.

His son Kol rode up with a small group of soldiers. There was a dozen or so of men tied behind their horses.

"Deserters, father!" His son had a cruel grin on his face. Feng took him aside, and whispered:

"I don't know how much longer I can control this army of mercenaries – there will be more deserters. We must act soon." He looked at the prisoners in disgust. They were very young, pale and terrified. Feng turned to the soldiers. "Hang them."

As he rode off he pulled his cloak around him – it was growing ever colder.

Chang was weary. He lay back and closed his eyes, and before long he was dreaming …

He was a young officer again, training for command, and had fine reports from his mentors and superiors.

Shortly after Fu had been named Emperor, Chang had been given time to visit his parents in the tiny village of Ule. News had reached him of a wandering storyteller who would arrive at the Peacock Inn at sundown. These storytellers were highly respected in the villages, and Chang had always loved to listen to their splendid tales, which they told in taverns and inns where they were given free ale and a bed for the night.

When evening came he made his way to the inn and sat waiting with the other villagers, slowly sipping his ale. As the hour grew late they were about to give up on their guest when a traveller's step was heard outside the door, which, after a pause of a few moments, suddenly swung open, and there, silhouetted against the night, stood the strange figure of the storyteller.

He was of no particular age, with an unkempt beard and a mass of red-brown hair. He was plainly dressed in traveller's clothes and a large floppy hat, and he spoke in a peculiar accent that Chang could not place. "I've left my poor tired donkey in yonder barn – could somebody take care of him?"

The storyteller was welcomed and given a chair by the fireplace and strong ale to drink. For a time, he was silent, and then, having supped his full, the storyteller put down his glass and began: "Many years ago, when I was but a child ..."

All were captivated. His stories were vibrant and full of life. There were several sad tales that made the young women weep, but he always followed these with a merry, preposterous story which filled the inn with raucous laughter and cheer.

Finally, the storyteller ended his tales, and was loudly applauded as he retired for the night. Chang made his way to the stables and was about to saddle up when the mysterious storyteller appeared before him. Wordlessly the storyteller took off his hat, pulled the wig of red hair from his head, and removed the fake beard. Chang was struck dumb – for there in front of him was the Emperor Fu, grinning from ear to ear. "Sire!" Chang attempted to bow, but Fu caught him in an embrace and whispered.

"No kneeling here – I am but a humble storyteller! You, however, are now the Commander of the Emperor's Guard, and will report to the palace at your earliest convenience! Here – this is one of my favourite stories." And he handed Chang a scroll, tied with silk ribbons. "See you soon, Commander." And with this, Fu re-fixed his disguise, gave a solitary wave, and patiently led his stubborn donkey off into the night. When Chang opened the scroll, he saw it was his official commission, personally signed by the Emperor, and for a moment tears filled his eyes.

They were still there when Chang once more pulled on his clothes, and prepared to face another day of siege.

✸

"Curses on them! How many more must we hang?"

Lord Feng was enraged. He called his son to him. "This has gone on long enough! If they have not surrendered the city by dawn, burn it down – all of it!"

He knew he was beaten, but at least he would have his revenge on the city of Qan.

✳

Behind the bar of The Seafarer's Inn, Mr. Po lit his pipe and watched the Net-weavers at work. The three women sat huddled in a corner and kept their own company, patiently repairing torn canvas and shrouds.

The inn's proprietor, however, was becoming increasingly irritated as the siege wore on. The blockade was crippling business in the harbour, and Lord Feng's patrolling warships were making everybody nervous.

He cast his mind back to the funeral of the Emperor Fu. The Seafarer's Inn had been closed in respect for the passing of the Emperor. Mr. Po had stood solemnly outside as the procession reached the inn, and the entire works of the harbour had stopped, the banners of the ships at half-mast. As the procession approached the docks the ships had started to let off their sirens, first one at a time, and then in unison, as if a huge wail of grief had suddenly called out from the very ocean itself. Mr. Po had only shed tears once before in his long and colourful life, but on Fu's passing, he had lowered his head and wept like a child.

As he recalled that day, Mr. Po grew restless. However, before he could devise any plans, a young girl burst into the bar and shouted, "Mr. Po! Mr. Po! Something is happening in the harbour!"

By the time Mr. Po reached the dock-side the battle was over. One of Feng's warships was sinking under an immense barrage of arrows and fire. The two remaining ships were attempting to flee, but were unable to manoeuvre in the confined space of the docks. The two ships were being forced closer and closer together until … with a sickening grinding and wrenching sound – they rammed into each other.

Mr. Po was shocked, the blockade had been lifted! But who could have done this? Before he had time to speculate, a fleet of ships began to appear in the harbour. They were beautiful sleek vessels with tall masts and white sails. They were so fast, so agile, and so many, that Feng's heavy warships stood no chance against them.

✳

Chang had been sleeping fitfully when the dream came to him.

He was walking through a park lined with swaying trees and strange flowers of rare beauty. And there, seated on a bench, looking out across a calm glassy lake, was the Emperor Fu. Fu rose to greet him, and after their embrace they sat together, and the Emperor began to speak:

"Chang, my friend, you have always had faith in me?"

"Always, Sire."

"Then trust me once more. You must ride out at dawn and face the enemy. It is the only way to save Qan."

"Sire?"

"Even now Lord Feng and his warriors are planning to raze the city to ashes if they cannot take it intact."

"Sire, we are seriously outnumbered. In open battle they will crush us from all sides."

Fu nodded. "It would seem so, but remember – battles are won and lost by the element of surprise – by choosing when to fight and when not to fight. Feng's weakness is his arrogance. He will not expect you to attack."

"But they will see us ride out, and they will know how few we are."

"Have faith. A snowstorm approaches from the north. By dawn they will not be able to see you clearly, and will not be certain of your numbers. Now listen. I don't have much time ..."

Chang woke abruptly. Had the dream been a real message, or was it just his tired mind playing tricks on him? All his instincts were against riding into battle so badly outnumbered. He was about to dismiss the dream as only a strange fantasy when, as he buckled on his sword, he looked out from the tower. Across the fields, in the distance, a light snow was beginning to fall.

In the quiet of the Seafarer's Inn the youngest of the Net-weavers let out a gasp and held out her hand. A small pool of blood was forming where her needle had slipped.

Chang had made his decision. It was all or nothing now. Captain Yan smiled broadly. "We're almost ready sir, let's beat them back to where they came from!"

"I know we are taking a risk, Captain, but I would rather die on my knees than see Qan burn."

Chang rode slowly towards the city's iron gates as his soldiers began to amass behind him. He was never one to make speeches before a battle, but he held up his sword, and looked around at the crowd of frightened people who had gathered to show their support. Some families were huddled together, the children dumbfounded, and some of the old men were holding staffs and staves. The women had embroidered the emblem of Qan on a huge tapestry draped over the battlements, and the ancient blue sea-dragon looked on menacingly.

Chang raised his sword higher. "For Qan!" He shouted. And the soldiers and the crowd echoed. "For Qan! For Qan!"

Chang approached the iron gates. Huge chains began to turn, and Chang and his soldiers rode out.

✳

Lord Feng had been caught off-guard, but his forces were re-grouping. As the snow-storm cleared, the two armies engaged. Feng's large charger ran riot through the chaos, his sharp sword slicing and cutting down soldier after soldier. But this was no way to fight. He could barely make out friend from foe – and then he caught sight of Chang, who had been unhorsed and was fighting hand-to-hand. Feng brutally despatched anyone in his path. When he reached Chang, he dismounted. Chang swung around and their eyes locked. Feng smiled grimly. "It's between us now, Chang."

"It always was," Chang replied, and their swords clashed …

Chang had the swiftness and the skill, Feng had the strength and durability. Chang thought he could outlast his opponent by swerving and ducking beyond the reach of Feng's lethal sword. Equally Feng knew that if he could land but one blow, the fight would be over.

Neither of the men gave any ground, but circled each other like hungry wolves. They paused for breath, and Chang saw his chance and lunged at Feng, but Feng lurched to one side and aimed a crushing blow at Chang when he was off-balance. Chang tried to swerve again, but this time he wasn't quick enough, and the tip of Feng's sword opened his cheek and sliced into his arm and leg …

Chang felt no pain, only a cold, savage fury, and he leapt at Feng with renewed strength and recklessness, battering his shield until it was completely torn away. Feng tried another swing with his heavy sword, but he was too slow, and Chang drove his sword under his ribs and into his heart. Feng staggered a few steps and fell on his knees. He was dead within reach of the iron gates.

Chang's rage left him, and he could barely stand, but he could see that his cause was lost. His soldiers were being beaten back towards the gates, overwhelmed by superior numbers. With the last of his strength he re-mounted his horse and rode into the thick of the battle. His sword found shield, armour, flesh and bone, and in return his body became a mass of wounds and pain he could not feel. Before he fell he thought he saw fresh riders approaching, but he was unconscious before he could make out their colours.

Slowly Chang opened his eyes and lifted his head. All around him the wounded were being attended to by ... warrior women he did not recognize. As he tried to sit up one of the women leaned over him.

"No, no! Keep still." She applied some salves and ointments to his wounds. "You were very lucky, Commander."

"Who are ...?"

"I am called Sharisha. Do not try to move." She examined Chang's wounds again, and then called out. "Lady, he is awake."

Through the mist an incredibly beautiful young woman appeared on horseback, riding serenely towards them. Unlike the other women she wore no armour, but over her muddied dress was draped a strange black cloak that was full of stars, held in place by a golden half-moon emblem. As she drew nearer, Chang noticed the stars were constantly fading and re-appearing.

Before he could form any thoughts, she addressed Chang in a clear calm voice. "Well, Commander, it appears you will live." She seemed almost amused, but then her tone changed to one of anger.

"I am the sorceress Meili. Feng's warships have been destroyed, and my warriors have decided the battle in your favour. Now, I have only one question for you – where is my father?"

It was late, and after a long night the Seafarer's Inn had finally closed its doors. Mr. Po poured himself a drink and sat down at one of the tables. Within minutes his eyes were closed and he was drifting.

Once again, he saw the fleet of ships with billowing sails, saw again Lord Feng's warships crumbling into the sea, and heard the lonely cry of the seagull circling above.

The vision faded, but then he heard a voice, a very weak voice calling from a distant place, a prison, perhaps – but where ... where?

Mr. Po woke with a start. He stood up slowly, and carefully weaved his way between some barrels. For some time, he studied a sailing chart that was fixed to the wall behind the bar. And then he nodded to himself and reached for his pipe.

"The Haunted Isles," he muttered under his breath. "Of course!"

Part 3: The Voyage

Meili sighed in exasperation. It seemed to be taking forever to prepare and provision the three fastest ships in the fleet for the voyage ahead. The choice of captains had been much easier. Mr. Po, who had a lifetime of experience at sea, would captain the *Flamingo*, Captain Yan would command the *Nightingale*, and Commander Chang would captain her flagship, the *Sea Eagle*.

Meili smiled at herself. Some sorceress she'd turned out to be! She hadn't an inkling of where her father was being held captive until the enigmatic Mr. Po had arrived suddenly at the palace and told them of his vision – The Haunted Isles. When she had cast a searching spell across the water she had picked up a very faint sending, but she was desperately worried. If it was her father, his sending had been so weak and unstable ...

A growing frustration at the irritating delays gnawed at her. She was at the point of screaming out loud when there was a quiet knock on the door. She turned around sharply. "Yes!" The door swung open and Commander Chang ducked under the beam.

"The tide is with us now, my lady. I've just given the order to sail."

✳

Kassion's strength had almost gone. The cold grew deeper and it was harder to breathe. In his sleep he heard voices from the past, laughter, tears, fragments of conversation – and then the long unendurable silence of wakefulness. Regrets plagued him. Hope had run its course, and soon it would be over, unless …

A chink of light from somewhere, and the echo of a footstep. And then a gruff voice outside his cell:

"Get him on his feet – and clean him up – make him ready for trial."

✳

Aboard the *Flamingo* Mr. Po studied the ancient charts laid out before him.

They had sailed from the city of Qan past the Dragon Isles and were now heading north towards the Isles of Stone. Beyond this, all was treacherous.

The Zan-tu Archipelago was made up of three large islands – the Southern Lands, the Great Su Desert, and the largely uninhabited Frozen Lands in the north. Smaller island groups were dotted around each of the larger islands, and The Haunted Isles was the most northerly of these, lying off the east coast of the Frozen Lands. Mysterious and legendary, the waters around them were notoriously perilous. Mr. Po had heard tales of giant sea monsters, dragons, and huge whirlpools impossible to sail around. And if that wasn't enough, there were whispers and murmurings of the dreaded Lake of Blood.

This fearful stretch of water encircled the Haunted Isles and supposedly carried the blood of every mariner who had perished at sea, and whose soul had been weighed by the sea-gods and found wanting. Pirates, brigands, mutineers and murderers all. And yet, the sea-gods were known to be fickle …

Mr. Po was not a superstitious man by nature, and paid little heed to hearsay or myth, and yet he felt a certain apprehension as he lit his pipe, poured himself a glass of wine from a dusty bottle, and leaned over the charts again.

Kassion was seated in the middle of a large white courtroom. The ceiling was high and the court was sparsely decorated, save for two beautifully embroidered tapestries that hung from the wall behind a raised dais where the judges sat. The embroideries were clearly the emblem of his people – two half-moons facing each other, surrounded by the ever-changing stars.

Here Kassion faced the Dream Merchants.

He recognized all of his accusers. Five of them sat in a semi-circle, the highest seat in the centre, facing him. To the right sat the granite-faced Mur, with his hawk-like eyes and stormy temper, and next to him the beautiful and mystical Herla, a woman so gracious and desirable, yet so terrifying when angered. To the left sat the formidable Viska. Some said she was a goddess who had existed before time itself, so great were her powers. And then there was the enigmatic Crel, who always seemed distant and rarely spoke. But just taking his place on the centre chair of the Ruling Council was Kerilos, his eyes and senses taking in every action, every movement around him. Kerilos was tall and lean. His cloak was the colour of night, and his face showed the lines of age, but also of courage, determination and wisdom.

As the galleries began to fill with others of his race, Kassion looked around him. *Not so many of us left,* he thought, and a bitter sadness filled his heart. Kerilos' eyes had not left Kassion since he entered the courtroom, and now he spoke in a deep and clear voice:

"Kassion of the Star Homeworlds, you are here before us accused of the most fundamental crime of our race – you have deliberately interfered with the balance of eternal life. We will hear your plea. Our judgement will be final."

"Captain, we are under attack!" Chang hurried to the quarter-deck, his eyes wide in disbelief. A huge squid-like creature with monstrous tentacles was assailing the *Sea Eagle*. Chang rushed forward and, drawing his sword, sliced off one of the creature's flailing tentacles, but another lifted him and flung him across the deck into the guard-rail. Sailors panicked as the beast's tentacles writhed and grasped at the ship, tearing away the lifeboats and jib before it slid back into the water.

For several moments the sea was eerily still, but suddenly the creature rose up in front of the *Flamingo*. Chang could only watch in horror as it grasped the *Flamingo*'s prow and tried to pull her under. Just as it looked as though the *Flamingo* would be lost, Mr. Po appeared on the foredeck and, with a mighty cry, hurled his gleaming cutlass at the beast. The monster slowly loosened its grip on the ship, and then with an awful groan it fell over the side and into the depths.

Loud cheers resounded from all three ships, but on the deck of the *Flamingo* Mr. Po looked downcast. His first mate approached him, beaming with wonder and relief. "A splendid hit, Captain, but why so glum?" Mr. Po turned and tapped out his pipe on the foremast. "I was mourning the loss of my cutlass. It was a particular favourite of mine."

For long moments Kassion felt the eyes of an entire race upon him. There were whisperings and murmurings around the courtroom until Kerilos lifted his hand for silence:

"I will read the list of charges. Kassion – you are accused of taking a human child from a field of battle and raising her as your own. You are also accused of dream-sending and creating illusions from which the consequences are still unknown. Not only this, but you deliberately sent vision messages to a 'sorceress' who we now know to be your half-daughter, to assist in a siege that was no concern of ours. There are other minor offences, but you must answer for these grave transgressions and misuse of your powers!"

As the accusations were read out Kassion found himself growing angry. By the time Kerilos had finished he was irate. He stood and faced his accusers.

"To begin with – I rescued an orphaned child starving to death on a battlefield – because of a war *we* created!" Mur rose and interrupted.

"We are not responsible for every ..."

"But we *are* responsible! She was an innocent – a victim of our own actions when we crushed the Yurten Empire."

"In order to preserve the universal balance!"

"If it takes a starving child to 'preserve the universal balance', then the balance isn't worth preserving!" Kassion's eyes were burning with fury. "I saved the child Liena and brought her up as my own – and I would do the same thing again – yes, I am guilty!"

At this the noise from the galleries grew louder, but before total mayhem and disruption could ensue, Kerilos rose, and his voice carried command:

"Silence! Enough – this court is now in recess!"

After their encounter with the strange sea creature, the three ships sailed on past the Isles of Stone into dangerous waters. The sea was becalmed, and there was no wind to tell of. Aboard the *Flamingo*, the sailors were restless.

"I don't like it, Captain." The boatswain was a veteran of many voyages.

"No, it's too quiet." Mr. Po cast his eyes over the ship. "Take down the mainsail. Message the flagship – we must row."

Kassion had resumed his defence:

"I make no apology for rescuing the child Liena from the battlefield. As for the dream-sending, the dreams were already there, I merely drew them together, so they might find each other. The Castle of Rainbows – it may have been an illusion, but it was real enough for them – and for me. Besides, I am not the only one here guilty of casting illusions." There was an uneasy exchange of glances.

Kassion paused. "My half-daughter Meili ... I could never acknowledge her, for her mother was a human woman, who was killed in the bloodshed of Yurth. I left Meili in the care of others and watched her grow from afar. She knows nothing of me." He struggled on. "I sent her a vision to save the city of Qan from disaster – but I know not if she heard. And Meili ... is not my half-daughter." His voice faltered. "She is my *daughter*, of my flesh, and of my heart." Kassion sank back into his seat. There was silence in the courtroom.

Kerilos rose from his chair. "We must think on this," he stated. Kassion said nothing, only sat, his head lowered on his chest. As his accusers began to leave the room, Kerilos turned.

"Kassion, be comforted. Your ... daughter *is* aware of her father. Even now she sails here to rescue you."

31

The ships were being rowed cautiously onwards, when, aboard the *Nightingale*, Captain Yan was called on deck. One of his lieutenants passed him a telescope. "Sir – look up ahead." One look was enough for Yan.

"Back! Turn back!" The skies were suddenly full of swirling black clouds, and the sea was churning, boiling and heaving. Spray from huge waves were blinding the crew. In the growing darkness, the young lieutenant pointed in horror –

"The maelstrom! The maelstrom!" It must have been over a mile in diameter, its vortex unfathomable – and the *Nightingale* was being drawn relentlessly towards it.

The *Flamingo* was listing dangerously. Mr. Po was yelling, trying to make himself heard above the howling wind and spray. "Lash yourselves to something – anything – and row your hearts out!"

The *Sea Eagle* was desperately battling against the strong current. One of the sailors collapsed on his oar, and Chang clambered over the deck to take his place. "Row! Row! We must make open water – row!" He looked up at the sky. Huge masses of clouds were forming, and torrents of rain began to lash the decks. As he lowered his gaze he saw Meili, her arms raised above her head, chanting against the wind. The sea raged and the storm ripped the rigging from the mainmast and tore through the shrouds. And then to his utter dismay, Chang caught a glimpse of another ship through the tempest. "The *Nightingale* – she's sinking!"

A resounding clap of thunder broke overhead, and forks of jagged lightning lit up the skies. The *Nightingale* was caught in the whirlpool, and could not escape. Slowly and inexorably, she was pulled down beneath the foaming waves, and all were powerless to prevent it.

✳

Kassion had nearly collapsed on hearing the news of his daughter. Despite reassurances, he was overwrought. Eventually he was given a sleeping draught, and Kerilos covered him with a blanket.

"Have no fears. Rest, and regain your strength."

✳

The *Sea Eagle* and the *Flamingo* moved in towards the edge of the Lake of Blood. Using the telescope, Chang could just make out land on the other side. "No one's ever crossed it," he said to himself, but Meili was standing beside him.

"We are so close."

The first officer approached. "Mr. Po sends word that he has found a narrow channel to the north of the islands, but it will take several days to sail around the lake to reach it."

Meili cried out in anguish. "We don't have several days! I can feel how weak my father is. We may already be too late."

Chang shared her frustration. "Can you use your powers to calm the lake enough for us to cross?"

"And risk all our lives? I failed at the maelstrom. I couldn't save the *Nightingale*." Her face was streaked with tears. "I couldn't save them ..."

Chang took her hands. "The maelstrom was too strong – there's nothing you could have done."

But Meili was inconsolable.

Slowly the ships sailed on, and slowly the water turned a dark blood-red.

It wasn't long before the voices began. They were faint at first, but soon their wailings echoed all around them. They were the voices of the dead, but they were not at rest, for their souls were caught in eternity's wheel, and could never escape.

"I am Davie Locke – I perished on the Phantom – attacked by pirates. They burned our ship, butchered us all …"

"I am Li Ho. They hanged me from the yardarm – but I was not guilty of the theft. They cast me into the ocean, the deep, dark waters …"

"I am Joseph Lord, Captain of the Guinea. We didn't see the black rocks in the dark, the ship split in two, my crew drowned, all drowned …"

Another voice, and another, until the sound of their tormented souls reached a crescendo of misery and despair. Most of the sailors were on their knees, trying to cover their ears, or praying to the sea-gods. The ships began to slide, the tide of the lake slowly dragging them off course. Aboard the flagship, Chang cried out to Meili:

"You must try. You must try!" Meili was weeping, but Chang held her face. "If you cannot stop them, we will all die here and now!"

Meili stood absolutely still. She closed her eyes and grasped the half-moon amulet that held her cloak around her. She began to chant, unsure at first, and then more steadily. The Lake of Blood churned beneath the ship, and began to hiss and spit red spray onto the deck. Meili continued chanting, but she could feel her weakness against the pull of the lake. A hopelessness filled her soul. She was drifting towards the edge of life, guided by a thousand desperate voices, towards the abyss.

She was being shaken, and Chang was pointing. Across the lake, on the far bank, stood five robed figures. Meili instinctively knew who they were. With calm deliberation each figure stretched out one hand towards the lake, and raised the other to the skies. The waters of the Lake of Blood howled and roared, threatening to drown them all in their unbearable lamentations.

Meili fixed her eyes on the five mages, who were now surrounded by a luminous glow, and, suddenly remembering the incantation, she hurled the spell across the waters. There was a horrifying scream from the lake, a terrible rending of desperation and fear, and abruptly, the voices were silenced.

✳

A light rain began to fall on the Haunted Isles, but the waters were calm again as the *Sea Eagle,* battered and torn, dropped anchor in a quiet cove. The *Flamingo* limped in behind her, and small rowing boats were pulled up onto a stony beach. Meili cast her eyes over the inhospitable landscape and turned to Sharisha. "I must find my father. I know he is here."

"I'll take you to him. Follow me." The voice had come from everywhere, but it was Kerilos who had spoken. Neither of the women had seen him approach, but he was standing only a few paces away. Sharisha was about to speak, but Meili hushed her.

Kerilos led them up a steep trail of steps, out of the cove, and across a wide yellow field. At the far edge of the field stood a circular white building that looked like it belonged somewhere else. Kerilos guided them through its doors and down a flight of marble stairs. Finally, he stopped outside a cell door which had no lock. "In here."

Meili gently pushed the door open. At first, she could see nothing. The room was completely dark until Sharisha handed her a lantern. In the corner of the room, huddled on the floor, was Kassion, shaking in fitful dreams. Meili knelt down beside him. She touched his face gently, and his eyes half opened. Her voice was barely a whisper. "Father, I'm here ... it's Meili ... Meili." She reached for her amulet, and held it against his, and the two half-moons became one.

✳

In the cloisters of the courtyard Mur was raging:

"So Kassion was set free – even though he dared to interfere with destiny!" Herla smiled, and looked unconcerned.

"And whose destiny are you referring to? The universe does not stand still – in order to survive even we must adapt. Perhaps Kassion made us look a little closer at ourselves – not entirely a bad thing." She smiled seductively, and with a swish of her cloak, she was gone.

✳

After resting for a week and refitting the ships, it was time to leave. The Dream Merchants had once more gone their separate ways but Meili and Kassion decided to return to Qan, where Meili's fleet was waiting for her.

Before they set sail a single piece of driftwood, bearing the name *Nightingale* was washed up on the rocky beach. A solemn vigil was held for all those they had lost. Meili could not restrain her tears as her father tried to comfort her. "We should not grieve for those who sacrificed themselves for us, but rejoice in finding such rare comradeship."

The *Sea Eagle* and the *Flamingo* sailed north from the Haunted Isles, around the Frozen Lands, and then due south. They navigated Witches Bay without incident, and stopped off briefly at Serpent City to take on fresh water and supplies. From there they sailed past the Western Isles into the warm and tranquil waters of the Southern Ocean, landing at Qan harbour on a fine summer night, with the distant stars looking down upon them.

Chang knew he was losing this particular battle. "Ridiculous! I'm no Emperor – I'm a soldier!"

"But the people are calling your name. You cannot abandon them now." Sharisha had just returned from the courtyard where a large crowd of people had gathered, calling for Chang to accept the throne he'd been offered by the city elders.

"But I told them all – I'm not of royal blood. I have no right ..."

"You have earned the right! There are none of royal blood left, and the people won't accept anybody else."

"But I don't know how – or where – to begin."

"Accept what is freely given. This is your time."

Chang was wavering. "I don't think I can do this ... alone."

"Then you will need a wife to patch up your endless wounds."

✴

It was a matter of days before Chang was made Emperor, and married Sharisha. In the streets the people rejoiced and celebrated. Chang's first decree was to announce a public holiday which lasted three weeks. The only moment of sadness was the departure of Meili and Kassion. Chang held Sharisha close as they stood watching Meili's fleet sail away into unknown seas. "They said they would return one day," Sharisha whispered.

"I hope so. She saved us all."

✴

That night, as Chang slept, he thought he heard the distant voice of the Emperor Fu. *Do you remember – when we were children – we both made a wish? Well, sometimes our wishes come true!*

✴

In his absence, Mr. Po had left his old friend Mr. Yu in charge of the Seafarer's Inn. Mr. Po was delighted to be home again. "Mr. Yu, I thank you most heartily for keeping the old place as I left it."

Mr. Yu placed a bottle of the finest wine on the table and poured out two full glasses.

As the inn began to fill once more with mariners, fishermen and other regulars, the two friends drank and talked long into the night.

In the quietest corner the Net-weavers continued their work, repairing the torn canvas and shrouds from the boats, and spoke not a word.

Frontiers
(A Tale of Ancient Rome)

Part I: Omens

The Isle of Britannia, Midsummer 405 AD

Caius felt the presence of the standing stones long before their eerie silhouettes appeared on the horizon.

"I feel I know this place. It seems … familiar, as if I've been here before …"

The centurion, Quintus Attalus, shook his head. "It looks like an ancient shrine – a place of worship or ritual. There are many who still hold the old gods sacred."

"But these stones are immense. Who could have built this?"

"I don't know, Caius, but it makes me feel uneasy. I think we should move on." Caius looked up at the shifting clouds.

"It will be dark soon, and we must rest the horses. Perhaps we can find lodgings for the night."

As they drew closer to the standing stones, their progress was halted by a large gathering of people – mostly villagers and craftsmen with their families, making their way along a well-worn track that led to the centre of the ring of stones.

Caius pulled up his horse. "Well, they look peaceful enough. Let's dismount and follow – we may learn something."

"I don't like it, Caius."

"We are in a foreign land, Quintus. We must not provoke any incidents. Besides, I am tired. This ritual – whatever it is, cannot take long, and then we can seek some supper, wine, and a warm bed for the night!"

Quintus still looked uncomfortable. "Very well, but you go on alone. I'll look after the horses, and try to discover if there is a village or town nearby." They dismounted, and as Quintus led the horses away, Caius allowed himself to be drawn into the crowd.

It was a slow procession, and many of the people around him appeared to be on the edge of exhaustion, as if they had been walking for days. Their feet were swollen and bruised, and their clothes dirty and in tatters. None of them bore any weapons, and Caius was very conscious of the short sword he always carried at his side. He was relieved that instead of their full regimental uniforms, they decided to opt for travelling clothes and cloaks, but even so, he felt somewhat awkward and out of place.

Caius had always been curious about local customs, and he was strangely drawn to these standing stones. He felt as if something significant was about to happen, and that fate was about to roll its dice again. An old man beside him stumbled, and Caius helped him back onto his feet and handed him a flask of water. The old man was loosely clad in weathered rags, and his beard was long and unkempt. His hair fell down over his eyes, and yet he spoke clearly, with an educated manner. "Thank you – oh, you are not one of us – are you sure you belong here, my friend?" Caius hesitated, but could find no response, so he asked:

"Who are these people, and why do they flock here?"

"They come to offer sacrifice to the old gods, to see the new sun rise, and to hear the prophecies. It has been a long pilgrimage for some. This is a most sacred place, but you – Roman – why are you here?"

"In truth I cannot tell you, but for some reason I knew that I had to follow."

The old man smiled. "Who can tell what the gods have in store for us? It is all a mystery – I wish you well – Roman." And with that he turned away, and began to join in with a low murmuring chant that was arising from the pilgrims.

They slowly advanced towards the centre of the ring of stones. Caius could see that some of the stones were laid out as an altar, and stained with dried blood. The chanting grew louder around him, and many of the pilgrims fell to their knees in supplication or prayer.

The setting sun was creating beaming patterns of light around the stones, and a strange force or power seemed to emanate from them. Caius felt an overwhelming tide of weariness upon him, as though he were being lulled into a deep sleep.

Suddenly a loud drumming filled the air, and five beautiful young women appeared around the altar stones. They all wore long white dresses, and flowers in their hair. Each of them led a tethered goat towards the centre stones. From out of nowhere, a sixth woman appeared, clad in the robes of a high priestess. She too was beautiful, but stern of face and manner. On either side of her stood two muscular guards, holding spears and bearing themselves as warriors. The priestess began to chant in a language that Caius could not understand. He felt a peculiar dizziness, and then he heard her voice clearly in his head, speaking directly to him:

"Caius Antonius, your fate has been decided among the gods. Soon you will be leaving these shores to follow your destiny. But you must beware, for the ghost of Remus haunts the Romans – his blood still pours from open wounds! Your faith is like the ashes of a phoenix that does not have the strength to rise. You fight ... against yourself – you will lose and you will win. You will sin and yet be cleansed. Mercy and freedom – freedom and love – love and desire – you will never return to these sacred isles!"

Cauis' mind was reeling, and he could not steady himself. The last thing he remembered as he fell was the long knives tearing at the goats' throats, and fresh blood pouring over the sacrificial stones, staining the earth beneath.

It was morning. Caius opened his eyes and looked around. He did not know where he was. His head ached as if he had been drinking too much wine the night before, but he knew this was not the case. He began to dress himself, and he was trying to piece together what had happened, when there was a knock on the door and Quintus appeared, looking concerned. "Caius, how are you? I have been worried – you seemed delirious."

"Quintus, how did I get here, where are we?"

"I looked for you when the crowd dispersed, but I couldn't see you. I asked some men to help me search, and we found you unconscious and carried you back to the horses. They told me there was a tavern in the village where you could rest, so I brought you here – Caius – what happened?"

Caius resumed dressing. "I remember a lot of chanting, a strange priestess, and then I felt dizzy – I must have passed out." Caius was being evasive. He didn't wish to discuss the prophecy he had heard. He was a trained Roman soldier – a tribune who was used to giving orders and organising men into efficient fighting units. Besides, he and Quintus had been stationed in Britannia for the last three years, and they were about to re-join their regiment in Londinium.

It had been a glorious summer, and the sun was already breaking through the clouds. They sat downstairs in the empty tavern, enjoying their breakfast. Caius was about to dismiss his experience the previous evening as a result of tiredness and too much imagination, when a young boy arrived at the tavern and asked the innkeeper for him by name. "Over here son, I'm Caius."

The boy passed him a sealed scroll, and after receiving the customary coin, scampered out of the inn. As Caius read through the scroll he grew increasingly agitated. Quintus gripped his shoulder. "What is it Caius – something wrong?" Caius handed the scroll to Quintus.

"We have to leave – we're not going back to Londinium. The entire legion has been ordered to Germania – we've been ordered to the frontier."

Part II: Pit of Vipers

The Rhine/Danube frontier, mid-December 406 AD

The ambush had been well planned. The barbarians had attacked at first light, and the fighting was brutal and vicious. Caius had felt his life was over more than once. He fought back with recklessness and anger rather than any great skill. The enemy were fearless and savage, and all his training had counted for nothing in the utter mad fury of the fight. Eventually the Romans had re-grouped, formed a shield wall, and pushed the barbarians back until they retreated and fled.

Caius was accustomed to war and suffering, but he knew these continual skirmishes were taking their toll. How many men had they lost this time? The barbarians were growing stronger, and it was becoming more and more difficult to hold them back. Caius sighed and wiped his sword.

"Tribune – Caius!" The blood-soaked centurion broke into his reverie, saluting through his weariness and relief. Caius surveyed the battlefield.

"Quintus, we cannot withstand another attack."

"Sir, we are not far from the fortress now. Two more days, at most."

"That's good, Quintus, but we cannot loiter here. We must reach the fortress. Where is the *legate*?"

"Dead, sir, he took an arrow in the throat. You are in command now."

For several moments Caius was silent, but there was no time for grief. "How many men have we left?"

"Around a hundred, and about thirty wounded. There were far more of the enemy than we expected in this area. They just came out of nowhere ... the rocks, the trees ..."

Caius nodded. "Out of the very land itself."

Just as they were preparing to march, a young soldier approached Caius and saluted. "Sir, we've got one of them trapped in a snake pit. He refuses to surrender."

"Very well – lead the way."

The barbarian warrior was young. He glared back at Caius defiantly. The pit was deep and impossible to climb out of, unaided. The vipers were coiled in a corner, barely moving. The young barbarian seemed indifferent to his fate, a lifetime of hardship and stoic teachings enabling him to accept his death without emotion. He hadn't been bitten yet, but it was only a matter of time. Caius took all this in at a glance and turned to one of the men. "Find some rope and pull him out."

"But sir!"

"That's an order, soldier!"

A rope was lowered and the young warrior carefully tied it around himself. As they began to haul him up one of the serpents uncoiled and struck at him, barely missing his trailing leg. When he reached the top of the pit the soldiers eyed him suspiciously, but brought him before Caius, who was helping to load one of the supply wagons. "Here is the prisoner, sir."

The young warrior was tall, with long straw-coloured hair, light blue eyes, and a mischievous grin. He seemed unconcerned that he was a captive of the Roman army. For a long moment a hush fell around the camp. "So," Caius spoke quietly. "You refuse to surrender?"

"I refuse. So, what now, tribune? Will you execute me, or throw me back into the pit?"

Caius was surprised. Despite his rugged appearance the barbarian had spoken confidently and had recognized Cauis' rank immediately.

"What is your name?"

"I am Anzo, son of Otto, the chieftain of our people."

"Well, Anzo, I have seen enough bloodshed today, and I have no use for prisoners. You may leave – on foot, with no weapons." It was Anzo's turn to be surprised.

"I … thank you, tribune, and I will not forget."

Caius drew his short sword and cut the warrior's bonds. "Now go – before I change my mind."

The young barbarian was led away, escorted out of the camp by two soldiers. Caius continued to load the wagon, carefully wrapping the regiment's eagle in a blanket. He was interrupted again as Quintus rode up. "Why did you free him, Caius?"

"No warrior deserves to die like that, not even our enemies."

Part III: Sub Rosa

The Rhine/Danube frontier, mid-December 406 AD

The sky had turned dark, and a cold wind swirled as they pitched the tents and made camp near a small stream. Caius whispered to Quintus. "Tell the men to keep their fires low, and post guards around the camp."

The moon was high when Quintus entered the command tent and found Caius resting on one of the cots. Caius rose to greet him, and Quintus was shocked at how tired he looked. Caius motioned for Quintus to sit. "It's been a long day. I thought we were done for this morning. Here, try some wine." Quintus nodded his thanks.

"It was yet another hard battle, Caius, and the men are tired. They fought bravely today."

"We've had one ambush after another since we got here, Quintus! Morale is low, and some of the men are questioning why we're here at all."

Quintus stood and began to pace up and down in exasperation. "Did we learn nothing from Adrianople …?" He cursed and flung his arms up in the air, but eventually he regained his composure and sat opposite Caius. Then he started to speak:

"Adrianople – I was there, Caius. A young foot-soldier full of the glory of Rome!"

Quintus sat back in the shadows. "We marched towards the barbarian encampment, so confident of an easy victory – until we saw their line of wagons, stretching out endlessly into the distance. We formed two lines, cavalry and infantry. The Goths lined up against us on the high ridge – we could not guess their numbers. It was incredibly hot, and we were low on water. The Goths set fire to the surrounding countryside and fanned the flames to increase our distress. They sent negotiators to deliberately delay the fighting – their reinforcements were much closer than ours, and we were growing nervous and impatient, waiting for the battle to commence.

"We never knew who gave the order, but our archers had attacked somewhere on the flank and had been routed by sheer weight of numbers – our soldiers were retreating in blind panic, running from the Gothic hordes. The barbarians charged us as our cavalry fled. Before we knew anything, we were surrounded, our flanks were unprotected and they drove right into us. The sky was full of arrows – and the noise! Men and horses screeching and yelling, swords whirling and shields clashing, and all the time the unbearable heat … it was a living hell! They forced us back and back – there was nowhere to go, there was no time, no room to fight. Terror overwhelmed us. We were being crushed to death, butchered and massacred like animals! I saw so many men cut to ribbons that day, without even a chance to defend themselves or fight back, and all I could think of was 'why?' Why had the gods abandoned us? And I found no answer, but heard only the mocking jests of our enemies as they tore us to pieces. It went on and on, relentless and cruel. We tried to hold our ground but it was no good – until finally – what was left of us – ran, Caius, we all ran!" Tears welled in his eyes and his voice broke. "Caius, it was nearly thirty years ago, and not a day goes by when I can forget."

For a while they sat quietly, and then Caius rose and placed his hand on Quintus' shoulder. "We break camp early. Try to get some rest."

"I'll check on the guards first." They clasped hands, and Quintus left the tent. Caius lay back and closed his eyes. The day had been a strain on his body and mind, but mostly on his nerves. He had so nearly been killed that morning. He vaguely remembered clashing swords with one evil-looking monster before a stray arrow had saved him, taking the man down before he could strike. Caius had injured his hand, and it was bleeding again, but he was too exhausted to change the dressing.

He was in command. He had to display leadership and strength to the men, had to stand apart and show no signs of weakness or doubt.

Caius was one of the youngest tribunes in the Roman army. His father had served before him, with distinction, and his father before that. But now he felt increasingly alone. He regretted the death of the *legate*, his commanding officer, who had been his friend, and he felt restless, as though something was wrong. Maybe it was just their situation. The Roman frontier forces, the *comitatenses* and *limitanei*, had suffered a series of heavy defeats from barbarian tribes of late, and many auxiliary units were scattered along the Rhine and Danube territories. They were disorganized, under-supplied and ill-equipped to deal with the increasingly dangerous barbarian incursions. Many of the forts and watchtowers were undermanned or neglected, and several of the legions had been re-deployed, or thrown into confusion after being cut off from the main field army. Caius shifted on his cot. His mind was going over the scene with the young warrior, trapped, alone, and facing death – but still proud and spirited, like other peoples Rome had subjugated. But what gave Rome the right to impose its will on other nations – the right of strength and military power – was that enough? Caius was no longer sure, but he must try to lead the company to safety, it was his duty ... the fortress ... his duty... to lead them to safety ... His eyes were heavy, and finally sleep overtook him and he drifted into the realm of dreams.

In his dream he was back home, in the Old Country, walking through the spring orchards with his younger sister, Claudia. The sun was shining and birds sang in the trees. He wore no armour, only a light toga, and Claudia skipped along beside him, pulling faces and making fun of him, humming a tune he remembered well from his youth. As they came in sight of the ancient house he heard his mother singing, and his father chopping wood, and he could smell the herbs and spices, and taste the sweetness of the wine upon his lips.

Caius turned in his sleep, and this time he saw a high half-moon, and a sky full of stars that flickered and faded, died and were reborn. Through the mist the priestess from Britannia was calling to him, beckoning him to draw closer. When Caius hesitated, she began to laugh and her beauty became twisted and cruel, like an ugly witch in a folk-tale. Her voice was bitter and harsh, and he turned his face away. He did not want to listen, yet her words played on his mind, and he could not escape. "You fight against yourself – you will lose! The ghost of Remus – open wounds – you will never return – never – never!"

Caius bolted upright, his heart pounding. By first light he was wide awake. When he left the tent there was a layer of snow underfoot, and the shrieking wind chilled him to the bone.

Part IV: The Black Forest

The Rhine/Danube frontier, late-December 406 AD

"I cannot see another way – according to our maps it would take at least three days to ride around it, and we have many wounded." Caius had called his two remaining centurions to him – Quintus and

Rufus, to discuss their situation. Both were veterans of many a hard campaign, but neither relished the thought of journeying through the forest up ahead.

Quintus wrung his hands together in frustration – and to keep out the numbing cold. "How many attacks have we already fought off? This forest is a perfect place for the enemy to trap us!"

Rufus was also concerned, and spoke in a hurried whisper. "We lost two more men in the night, and others worsened. Some may take the chance to slip away – they are frightened, tribune. We cannot watch all of them at all times."

"I know." Caius rubbed his chin, which was becoming thick stubble, and his injured hand stung in the rawness of the air. "Well, we have little choice – we cannot afford the time to go around the forest, we will simply have to ride through it and take our chances. Rufus – ride at the back of the column, and keep your eyes open. Quintus, let the men eat, and then get them ready – we've a difficult journey ahead."

Even the horses seemed to draw back as they entered the gloomy darkness of the forest. It felt as though they were trespassing into a mythical world – unknown, forbidding, and dangerous. They followed a narrow winding trail through the ancient woods. It was eerily silent. The canopy of tall trees blocked out the daylight, and all was covered in deep layers of freshly fallen snow.

At one point, Caius saw an archway through the trees, full of golden light, and a majestic stag standing serenely, observing them, as if guarding the doorway into a hidden kingdom. Caius stared until he was distracted by the snap of a twig nearby, and when he looked again, the stag was gone.

They continued on. The trail wore thin and then disappeared altogether. A wan moon could be glimpsed through the tree-tops, and the remaining light faded.

The men were alert to every movement behind every bush or rock, every shadow behind the trunk of a fallen tree. The silence grew oppressive – and suddenly the shriek of a bird could be heard crying overhead, and hands would instinctively reach for sword or spear. When all was calm once more they moved on again, after holding their breath for what seemed like an eternity.

It was not only the fear of an ambush by the enemy that made them all so nervous – it was the fear of an attack from wild beasts that hunted in the forest. Wolves could be heard in the distance, their piercing howls told of hunger and desperation. They hunted in large packs, and they were quick and clever, surrounding their prey and closing in with deadly precision. Huge bears also prowled in these woods. They were strong and savage creatures, and their onslaughts could be sudden and fatal. Snakes and lizards slithered and crawled through the undergrowth and along the branches of the huge gnarled trees, and it felt as though everything in the forest was watching them, waiting for them, and there was nowhere for them to hide, nowhere they were safe.

Some of the men had dismounted, their horses lame or too skittish to ride. In the heart of the woods a cart had become stuck, one of its wheels caught between two boulders, and it seemed like an age had passed before they could prise it loose. The wheel was broken and had to be replaced. Not a word was spoken as the soldiers surrounded the wagons, waiting interminably in the darkness before they could move on again.

Just as nerves were beginning to fray, Caius stopped and raised his hand for the column to halt. Quintus approached, looking pale and cold. Caius pointed ahead. The woods were thinning and they were emerging into a large clearing. "Look, old friend – the edge of the forest. Tell the men we're through."

Quintus sighed with relief.

Part V: Manoeuvres

The Rhine/Danube frontier, late-December 406 AD

They set up camp beyond the forest, and despite their fatigue, the company spent an uneasy night and got little rest. A thick fog had descended, and it was bitterly cold. The men huddled together around meagre fires, shivering in their cloaks. In the dead of night more snow began to fall, and the wind whistled and screeched through the tents. The lookouts returned, as visibility was too poor to make out friend or foe. The night dragged on. Caius lay on his cot with a bear-skin wrapped around him. He hadn't even closed his eyes.

At the first sign of dawn the order was given to break camp, and the wagons began to roll again.

Progress was slow as they marched on towards the fort. Caius led them, riding slowly, his horse picking a path through the treacherous snow and ice. The sky was white, and it was virtually impossible to maintain any pace or keep an orderly formation, as nothing could be seen through the grey curtain of mist. High above, carrion birds circled, and a wandering falcon soared, ceaselessly hunting for prey.

Finally, after what felt like an endless march, they reached the summit of a steep hill and could just make out the fort and its watchtowers in the distance.

Caius was leading the column forward, when suddenly the voice of the priestess invaded his mind. He was forced to dismount, clutching his head in anguish and pain.

The ghost of Remus – his blood still pours! The ghost ... the ghost ...

Quintus had quickly dismounted and was leaning over him. "Caius! Caius! What is it? What's wrong?" For some time, Caius could not answer, but slowly the priestess' voice faded, and the pain receded.

"It's nothing, Quintus – hurry now – we must keep going."

He stood again, but as the fog was clearing, his eyes made out a sight that unnerved him in an instant. All along the crest of the next hilltop, between themselves and the safety of the fortress – a huge barbarian army was waiting for them.

Time seemed to stand still, and nobody moved, as Caius and his small band of men looked on in disbelief at the numbers confronting them. They were experienced soldiers, and had survived against the odds before, but they all knew they could not win this time. Of the five hundred men of their unit, less than a hundred were still strong enough to fight. They were exhausted, hungry, and near to freezing. After all their efforts, their long struggle to reach safety had ultimately failed.

Quintus and Rufus joined Caius at the head of the column. Only Quintus spoke. "By all the gods, Caius – just look at them."

Caius said nothing, but only stared across at the enemy. Suddenly Quintus grabbed him by the arm and pointed. "Caius – look! Something's happening."

Caius watched as a small group of soldiers detached itself from the massive wall of the barbarian army and started to ride towards them. Rufus began to draw his sword, but Caius stopped him. "No, no! Wait! They want to talk. We must ride out to meet them."

Rufus snarled. "Why don't they just finish us off – they are toying with us!"

"Perhaps, but we must ride out – you and I, Quintus. We will talk with them. Rufus, I leave you in command. Do nothing until we return. If we don't return … your orders are to fight."

"I would have done that anyway – we will be ready for them!"

They rode out to meet the enemy. Quintus cursed the fates and then laughed. "Rufus is brave, but foolhardy. I hope he doesn't do anything rash."

"He is a good soldier, Quintus. He will obey orders."

"He was right about one thing – they could easily wipe us out. I wonder why they haven't attacked – what do they want?" Caius shook his head.

"We're about to find out."

The horsemen slowed as they drew near to each other, and there was hesitation on both sides until they finally stopped only a few paces apart. The horses snorted, and there was a heavy dampness in the air. Caius and Quintus made no move, but the leading horseman of the barbarians let go of his reins and slowly removed his helmet. Caius gasped in recognition of Anzo, the young warrior he had rescued from the snake pit. The barbarian warrior grinned, and leaned forward in his saddle. "So, tribune, once you had me at your mercy, now the tables have turned. We've been watching you for some time." Caius made no reply, but met the young warrior's steady gaze.

Quintus was reaching for his sword when Anzo spoke again:

"You allowed me to live, so I repay my debt to you – this once. In any case," and he glanced at Cauis' bandaged hand, "we do not make war on injured men. You may pass unhindered to your fortress, for what good it may do you. You have lost, Caius Antonius. Your great Roman army is weak and broken – you can hold us back no longer." Caius felt the truth of his words, but he replied angrily.

"We will fight on – to the very last man – you haven't won yet!" Anzo grinned again.

"It would only be a futile waste of lives, tribune. You cannot prevent the future any more than you can change the past, and now my patience wears thin. Go now, go to your fortress – we will not meet again." And with that Anzo turned his horse, gave a sharp order to his companions, and began to ride back to his army.

Caius and Quintus watched as the barbarians retreated and marched off, heading north.

Quintus was suspicious. "Do you think it's a trick, Caius?"

"I don't think so, Quintus. Like Rufus said, they could have finished us at any time, and I think young Anzo is a man of his word. Besides, we don't have much of a choice, do we?"

"Caius, how did he know it was you – how did he know your name – and how did they see us through all this fog and snow?"

"Please, Quintus, no more questions. I cannot give you an answer that makes any sense. There are mysterious powers at work – the priestess, the ritual – the prophecies ..." He hesitated.

"Caius, what are you saying?"

"I'm saying there are forces beyond our understanding or control, but I will not speak further of this – we must get the men into safety before nightfall. Enough talk, Quintus. We have been given our lives. Let us take the gift and be grateful for it."

They rode back to the column, where Rufus and several other soldiers were looking on. Rufus was dumbfounded.

"What happened out there?"

When Quintus had finished explaining, Rufus shook his head and stammered. "I can hardly believe it. They let us go ... we were bloody lucky." But as they advanced towards the fortress, a shocking sight awaited them. They pulled up their horses. Quintus whispered:

"Perhaps we were not so lucky after all, Caius."

Part VI: Frontiers

The Rhine/Danube frontier, late-December 406 to early January 407 AD

The fortress was almost in ruins. The outer walls had been breached in many places, several sections of the ramparts and battlements were beyond repair, and whole chunks of masonry and stone were missing from the towers. They waited. Eventually the gates were opened, but nobody rode out to greet them.

In the courtyard they dismounted, and Caius and Quintus looked around in horror at the devastation within. Rufus joined them, and put his hand across his brow. "This was chaos," he muttered grimly.

As the soldiers began to unpack the supply wagons, a pale-faced young officer emerged from one of the burnt-out buildings. He was followed by a small group of women wearing long cloaks and head-dresses. They immediately made for the rear wagons holding the injured soldiers, and began to help them off the carts and minister to their wounds.

The young officer approached them. He looked worn out, as though he had not slept for days, but he seemed relieved to see them. He saluted nervously. "I am Marius Varus, *signifer* of our legion. Forgive us, tribune, we couldn't ride out to meet you. We are somewhat in disarray, sir." The standard-bearer hesitated, and then continued. "Please, we can talk in the *principia*." He began to lead them to the building that served as the garrison head-quarters.

Walking through the fortress was a demoralizing experience. The barracks had fallen into a state of disuse and neglect, and many of the buildings were now only charred husks. The granaries were almost empty, the stables and workshops had been completely demolished, and the remaining cattle were thin and straggly. The armoury held no weapons of any use, and the hospital building was overcrowded with the sick and dying. Several women were acting as *medici*, trying their best to treat the wounded, but many would not last the night.

When they reached the *principia* they sat down at a long wooden table and the young officer poured them some wine. Caius' gaze fixed upon him. "Now, Marius, tell us everything." Marius cleared his throat and began to speak in a low, flat voice:

"When I first came here this place was thriving. We had food, livestock, and nearly six-hundred trained soldiers of the *limitanei*. We lived well, and were on friendly terms with the local villagers, who traded us horses, grain and warm clothing for the winter. We had two tribunes and five centurions, and we had no complaints."

He looked away, as if he did not wish to continue. Caius spoke evenly "What happened, Marius?"

"There was no warning, sir. They just attacked one morning and smashed through our outer defences with the first barrage from their siege weapons! Then their archers rained arrows of fire upon us. We rode out to fight them and … we lost nearly half our number before the barbarians retreated. When we returned to the fort many of the buildings were still afire. We struggled all night to extinguish the flames, but we were battered and leaderless. Both tribunes had been killed in the battle, and our centurions executed in front of us. The women and children … it was terrible, sir." Marius' head dropped. "All this happened half a year ago, and since then, I've tried my best, but …" His voice faltered and Caius saw the tears in his eyes.

"Steady son, go and get some sleep."

Marius left the three men and closed the door. For a while they sat in silence, and then Rufus slammed his fist down on the table, cursing loudly. He stood up, quivering with pent-up anger:

"It's over, Caius. Everything we've fought for. We've stretched the empire too far and lost control of it. We are tired, worn out – our legions are scattered, broken up, weak – and look at this young emperor, sitting in Rome and Ravenna, with his side-kicks and concubines, feasting and carousing while his soldiers die in the mud and the snow! We die, Caius, trying to hold a bloody, broken empire together – and the gods, if there are any – care nothing for us!" Caius stood to face him.

"Does that mean we fall upon our own swords? Do we just surrender and let the enemy take us? Enough, Rufus! We are soldiers.

We do our duty and we fight – we may question our orders, but we never lose our courage!" Rufus glared at Caius, growing red in the face with rage. His fingers touched the hilt of his sword, but Caius shook his head slowly. Finally, Rufus stormed out of the room in silence, leaving Caius and Quintus staring after him. Quintus spoke earnestly.

"He'll be all right, Caius. He's just exhausted and angry."

"We all are, Quintus."

That night Caius dreamed once more of the beautiful priestess. She seemed ethereal, real but unreal, physical yet incorporeal, young and yet ageless. She was seated on a throne-like chair in the centre of a large circular room with a high domed ceiling. They were alone, and all was quiet and still. Caius stood motionless. The priestess stepped down from her chair and approached him, her long robes brushing the stone floor. Caius was unable to take his eyes from her. He had so many questions … but he struggled to find any words.

"Who … are you?" he stammered awkwardly. For the first time the priestess smiled at him and her voice was calm and reassuring:

"I am called Viska by my people, and I dwell between your dreaming and your conscious mind." She moved closer to him. "Show me your hand." Caius held out his injured hand and sensed the warm glow of her touch, as if an enchantment had been cast upon him. Again, the priestess spoke.

"You have done well, Caius Antonius. There will be many battles ahead, and your road will be a long one, but overcome your doubts and you will prevail. Now, accept my gifts – and fulfil your destiny!"

When Caius woke, the pain in his hand was gone, and when he unwrapped the bandage his wound was completely healed. He wondered at this, but before he could reach any conclusions his eye was drawn to a strange amulet on a chain at the foot of the bed. It was oval shaped with a half-moon symbol etched upon it, made of a substance he did not recognize. It was not silver or gold but appeared to be a precious metal of some kind. He examined it closely and then placed it in a small box with a ring Claudia had given to him before he had left to join his regiment.

Caius thought of his family now – of his grey-haired parents who would no doubt be concerned at his long absence, and his little sister, now growing into womanhood, with her easy laughter and childlike pranks, and he wondered if he would ever see them again.

✳

Later that morning Caius and Quintus were walking around the perimeter of the fortress, trying to ascertain the extent of the damage. As they spoke together a messenger came hurtling towards them, riding his horse as if he were being chased by a thousand demons. Caius grabbed the reins of the leaping horse and tried to quieten the animal. He turned abruptly to the messenger, who saluted, and then began coughing and wheezing, trying to catch his breath. "Marcus Sabinus, sir. I rode through the night."

"Well, what is it? Speak up!"

"Barbarians, sir – further north – countless thousands of them. The tribes have joined forces and ride together. They crossed the river on the eve of the New Year."

"Crossed the river?" Caius was confused. "But how did they do this?"

"The river froze overnight – they just rode across. There was nothing we could do."

Quintus stared at the messenger, and then turned to Caius. His face was ashen when he spoke.

"Rufus said it was over – do you think he was right, Caius?"

Caius did not answer, but turned and looked into the distance as the icy wind blew from the north, stinging their faces, and once again, the snow began to fall.

Historical note

The 'barbarian' incursions (or migrations) of 406/07 did not immediately bring about the fall of the Roman Empire, but the pressure on the frontiers increased to the point where the Roman army could no longer control such a vast territory. In 410 the Romans officially withdrew their armies from Britain, and in the same year the city of Rome was sacked by Alaric's Visigoths. In 476 the Western Roman Empire collapsed when the last emperor, Romulus Augustulus, abdicated. However, the Eastern Roman Empire continued to thrive under various Byzantine emperors, until, in 1453, it finally succumbed to the forces of the Ottomans.

The legacy of Ancient Rome has survived, and still influences our culture, beliefs and philosophies today.

Darker

... and things have learnt to walk that ought to crawl

H.P. Lovecraft

I remember the terror – the sheer, screaming terror, and the sharp, tearing pain – followed by a cloudy numbness, and then, oblivion.

I was out cold for three days, and when I came round I had no idea who I was or where I'd come from.

They told me they had found me on a battlefield, and that I'd been injured in the leg and had suffered a violent crack on the skull, which probably accounted for my memory loss. We were somewhere in the north – Caledonia – and it appeared that I'd been a soldier, and that the rest of my regiment had been scattered or lost. Anyhow, I was the only one they had found alive, and I was covered in ashes, dirt ... and blood.

They'd rescued me from death – and given me a half-life.

I didn't believe any of it, of course. Didn't believe in 'the turning'. Werewolves, monsters – and vampires, all nonsense – I thought it was some kind of bad joke or childish game, and I felt only contempt and anger – until my gums ripped open and my mouth became an inferno of agony.

My 'saviours' were full of doubts about me. Their leader, Emilia, was a young woman, incredibly lovely, with long black hair and wonderful violet eyes. They told me she was the eldest, but I found that hard to believe. I felt drawn to her, but she was cold towards me, and would not speak.

✳

We travelled warily, usually after sundown or before dawn, on unused roads. We avoided the tinkers and traders in their ghostly grey wagons heading into the larger towns and villages to peddle their wares. We avoided the travelling circuses, with their roaring caged beasts and sad, lonely clowns.

I was still too weak to ride, so I lay huddled in the back of a horse-drawn cart with a blanket thrown over me to keep out the cold. My memory played subtle tricks with me. I saw only vague images of a past that I could not piece together – family, friends, the face of a woman I once knew – but nothing definite. Nothing I could be sure of.

I had once loved the sunshine, but now the sunlight stung my eyes, so I slept for most of the day, and suffered the most hideous dreams and hallucinations. Sometimes I would wake from these dreams raving and shouting, cursing God and all of His creations, until exhaustion overcame me or I was silenced by my companions.

There was one recurring dream which always left me feeling hollow and adrift ...

In this dream I was a hawk, eternally hunting, soaring high above the earth. Every creature feared me and fled from me. I ruthlessly attacked other birds, viciously tearing them apart in mid-air, and if I saw something move on the ground I swooped and fell on my prey like a bolt of lightning striking from above. I showed no mercy to any creature, but butchered all with equal efficiency and indifference. There was blood on my talons from so many kills, and still I continued hunting, unable to stop, unwilling to stop, until suddenly, from out of nowhere, an arrow pierced my wing, and I was falling, falling heavily and rapidly as though I suddenly weighed too much, and could not prevent myself from hurtling towards the hard, solid earth.

I tried with every breath in my body to stay in the air, but it was no use. I screeched and cried out, but only the huge stormy sky around me could hear my shrieks of terror. I hit the earth with a tremendous crash and felt the life slipping out of me, painlessly and pathetically, and there was nothing I could do, only lie there panting, fighting for air, but unable to breathe. But just when I thought my life had ended, I suddenly became the hunted, a small, docile creature, and looking up, saw the hawk, circling, hungrily. I desperately tried to crawl away into safety. I tried to hide, tried to find cover, but it was impossible, and the hawk circled once more, and swooped down upon me …

For some reason this dream disturbed me more than any of the others, the sequence repeating again and again, and I cried out in anguish, but there was no escape. On waking I was drained of all hope and energy, and I felt listless, beaten and worn out, as if I never wanted to move again.

✴

In my more lucid moments it seemed we were travelling through a haunted and desolate landscape. The trees were bare, the wind howled, and a dense layer of snow covered the ground for miles in every direction.

I had no name that I could recall, but one of the group had called me 'Reus', and as I could provide no other, the name had stuck.

It was a time of war. Everywhere we went we saw the dreadful aftermath of bloody battles and outright massacres. Fields were littered with the bodies of butchered soldiers and the rotting remains of horses and livestock. Some villages we passed through were empty, save for the mangled corpses of those who had stayed behind. The villages had been looted and burned, the people mutilated and murdered. It turned my stomach to witness such scenes, and we did not linger in these places, but moved on swiftly.

Eventually we found shelter in the ruins of an ancient castle on a hill-top overlooking a small village. It must have been a beautiful place once, with its serene views into the next valley, and the calmness of the tranquil ocean in the distance. I could smell the air, and the freshness of the sea breeze as never before.

But still I was an outcast, and I had never really understood what freedom was – until I became a prisoner.

At first, they locked me in one of the towers, but they knew I was too weak to attempt an escape, so after a while they left the door of my cell open, and allowed me to wander the grounds at night. Some nights I thought I heard the slow beat of drums in the distance – a monotonous rhythm – and dreadful wails, screeches, and chanting that taunted my imagination, but I could not be certain of anything in my condition, so I said nothing of this. I knew there was no point in trying to run, for where could I go? If I ventured inland the villagers would kill me on sight, and that vast blue ocean was far beyond my reach.

I also knew that I was being watched.

Some of the others had urged me to join the strange cocoon of their family, and told me how much I needed their strength and protection. One night they dragged in a human corpse – the body of an old man, a tramp – and insisted I fed. The battered swollen face and bruised limbs disgusted me, and despite my burning hunger, I refused and turned away, sickened and revolted by it all.

My night vision became clearer and sharper, and the pain in my mouth subsided. I'd survived up until now on small creatures, and sometimes birds, but this only seemed to make my hunger worse. The largest thing I'd taken was a young stray deer I found caught in a hunter's trap. It was pitiable, with a broken foot, dying slowly. I was ravenous, but even then I hesitated. I couldn't look at its face as I killed it with one twist of the neck. Its blood tasted warm and filled me with energy, but when I looked back at its small broken body I felt ashamed and impure. I returned to the tower and lay awake all night.

The next evening, two of the group visited me to tell me they were leaving soon, and that I must be strong enough to go with them, or it would end badly for me. I grew enraged and hurled abuse at them until they left, but the one called Alfonso stayed behind and spoke to me. He stood quietly by the door of my cell. He seemed troubled and on edge.

"Reus, have you heard strange calls in the night?"

"Yes, but I thought …"

Alfonso shook his head. "It is none of our doing. The villagers worship ancient gods. We've seen them sacrificing on their dark altars through the night. These are terrible gods, monstrous gods, gods of cruelty and torture – gods who promise no peace, no sanctuary – only war, torment and pain. The village elders turn the people against us because they are ignorant of our ways. They will come for us in their madness and hunt us down like animals!" Alfonso paced, trying to control his rising fury. "And they have priests – malicious priests who worship only evil. They perform their rituals and summon forth terrifying creatures from beneath the very pits of Hell!" He stopped, and then continued more deliberately. "These are unearthly demons, grotesque and twisted mockeries of human and animal form. They would enslave the entire world if they could escape from their confinement, but they are imprisoned by their own blind hatred of all, so that even Satan will have none of them."

Alfonso stopped pacing and looked straight at me. "They say that *we* have no souls, but I would not trade places with them for any price! We must leave this place, for it is cursed. It is a dark place, darker than any we've ever known." He placed a hand on my shoulder. "Brother, you either come with us, or you will be left to take your chances – alone."

When Alfonso had left, I sat down and pondered my options. I did not want to go with them, and yet, they were all the 'family' I had. I tried desperately to remember my past life, but it was a complete mystery, as if a veil had been drawn over my memories, blocking them out, and I could not see beyond it.

So, what was I going to do … go with them? I fidgeted in discomfort. And then my thoughts turned to my conversation with Alfonso. If the villagers were that dangerous it would be unwise to stay here alone and unprotected. It seemed like I had no choice, and despair was starting to creep up on me.

I lay down and tried to rest, tried to come up with some sort of plan to resolve my dilemma, but the more I considered the problem the more confused I got, and I could think of no solution. My body felt weak, and I knew that I couldn't go on like this for much longer. As time passed I seemed to be drifting into a dark and delirious madness. Again and again I heard the monotonous drum beats, and the sound seemed to stretch my ragged nerves as I paced the room, not knowing which way to turn, my hands covering my ears in an attempt to block out the awful drum beat. In my mind I could see the villagers tracking me down, old and young, men and women, with sinister grins on their faces, and long, reaching fingers ready to tear me to pieces. I saw the dreadful creatures Alonso had described, evil and vile, full of bitterness and disdain, clawing their way slowly and inexorably out of the horrid pit, moving towards me, never letting me go ... and I cried out in panic and fear until the visions dissipated into ghostly apparitions and faded into nothing. On and on this went, until my nervous energy left me, and my will-power was all but gone. I hungered worse than ever, and yet I was too exhausted and repulsed to think of food. My mouth was parched, and I was losing my grip on consciousness, fading, as if I was falling off the edge of something, into a deep, endless chasm of darkness.

Two nights later, I sat on my makeshift bed, shivering. My blood was racing, and I was constantly light-headed, cold and frightened. I felt lost and betrayed by the world. I could no longer tell the difference between illusion and reality, truth and lies. Whom could I trust anymore? I only wanted it to be over – to wake up out of this lurid nightmare.

Suddenly I heard the clock of the village church strike midnight, and somehow it sounded closer, more urgent, bleak and dismal. With the last of my energy I stumbled to my feet and opened the cell door – I had to get away! Slowly I staggered towards the spiral, winding staircase and step by step eased my way down. When I reached the foot of the stairs I looked around but saw nobody. I cast no reflection as I stumbled past the huge mirror hanging in the hallway. Panic gripped me and I stifled a growing scream of despair. I made a frenzied lunge for the main door – it was not locked, so I desperately pulled it open and almost fell into the courtyard.

The whole group were surrounding me. The flames from their torches flickered and leapt, creating strange shadows on the castle walls. An owl screeched in the night, and the stars seemed to glow and burn through the dark, windswept clouds.

They drew closer, and I saw they had a terrified young gypsy girl with them. Emilia took her by the wrist and pulled her forward. The girl seemed entranced, as if she was sleepwalking. She whimpered and tried to struggle, but could do nothing against Emilia's iron grip.

Emilia's beauty unnerved me, and suddenly her voice filled my head – strong, melodic, taking over my entire being. My heart beat faster, and my hands were shaking. I was caught like the deer in the trap. I longed for release, but Emilia's words were cold, and there was death in her voice:

"This is your last chance."

I looked at the gypsy girl and could barely speak. "Please, please … I can't … hurt her. I don't want to hurt her." Emilia exposed the girl's soft neck.

"Feed!"

"I can't do it – I can't *do* it!"

I fell to my knees, sobbing upon the dry earth, but Emilia lifted my face and stared into my eyes. Around her neck a half-moon amulet swung. I was paralysed by fear, but I could not turn away. Emelia knelt down beside me, cradling the gypsy girl as though she were a child, and for the first time, her voice softened.

"You must."

My mind closed on me. My senses were gone. I felt nothing. Saw nothing. My hand reached out towards the girl –

At sunrise, when the villagers and priests arrived, with their pitchforks, stakes and knives, they found no trace of us – only the bloodless remains of the gypsy girl, her pale dead eyes staring up in horror at a vast and turbulent sky.

The Ghost Moons of Zorandor VII

Part 1: Hard Lines

... commence broadcast ...

Group Announcement:

THE INTERPLANETARY GROUP WOULD LIKE TO ISSUE THE FOLLOWING STATEMENT: IT IS WITH DEEP REGRET THAT WE MUST REPORT THE LOSS OF THE PASSENGER FREIGHTER *HARD LINES*, ALONG WITH HER ENTIRE CREW AND COMPANY. THE SHIP WAS SHOT DOWN IN A COMPLETELY UNPROVOKED ATTACK BY THE FORCES OF THE UNDERGROUND MOVEMENT KNOWN AS 'THE DISSENTERS'. WE CAN ASSURE YOU, THE GOOD CITIZENS OF ZORANDOR VII, THAT THIS DISTRESSING ACT WILL BE MET WITH FULL REPRISALS. THE GROUP WOULD LIKE TO EXPRESS OUR SINCERE SYMPATHIES TO THE FAMILIES AND ASSOCIATES OF THE TWO HUNDRED AND SEVENTY-ONE INDIVIDUALS WHO PERISHED IN THIS DISTURBING INCIDENT. THE NAMES OF THE DECEASED WILL SHORTLY BE POSTED ON THE CENTRAL WEB, WHICH IS TEMPORARILY OFFLINE, AS THE SYSTEM IS UNDERGOING UPGRADING ENHANCEMENTS. HAVE A GOOD DAY.

... end broadcast ...

Meloney sat at the bar of the Wounded Dragon and watched the broadcast on the big screen. With a nod she ordered another drink, and placed a Group credit dialler on the bar. The surly bartender moved off to fetch the appropriate bottle. Meloney slipped away from the bar, through a small side-door, and into the warm and sultry evening air.

The Wounded Dragon was the oldest and most isolated inn on Zorandor VII. It was on the northern coast of Zol, and seldom used by city folk, although the place did a lively trade with all manner of travellers and those passing through on their way to Vellos. It was the last tavern before the ocean crossing, and attracted many sight-seers, as the views both inland and across the water were spectacular, being the highest point in the region. Its name alone inspired romance – the result of the old legend that the last dragon had perished on this very coastline, collapsing from exhaustion after flying across the entire ocean to escape her pursuers. Her bones, it was said, were still visible as the craggy rock formation on the peninsular, jutting out before the land gave way to the sea, where many a ship had been lost in the old days of sail.

Meloney felt her gaze being pulled along the coastline, and her mind was wandering, until she heard a beep from the communicator strapped to her wrist. The lined and care-worn features of her boss, Gilbert, appeared in unflattering 3-D clarity. As he leaned forward to speak, she could almost feel the man's tiredness like a living thing slowly devouring him.

Meloney was about to reply, when a harsh shriek of violent sound erupted in the sky directly above her, drowning out all other sounds. It was one of the Group's huge transport vessels, heading to the outer planets, carrying the most recent batch of 'volunteers' for the Army Defence battalions. There they would be trained as Group soldiers, in their seemingly endless war against the Fastillions.

The deafening sound lasted only a few moments, after which Meloney turned to her communicator and whispered to Gilbert:

"He's not here."

Without waiting for a reply, she clicked off the communicator and turned back to the Wounded Dragon to consider the options – and to finish her drink.

An hour later she tapped her glass, grinned at the scowling bartender, and left a large tip. She picked up her frayed denim jacket and headed for the exit sign, which flickered on and off, winking at the night with a neon battery eye.

✳

The great city of Zol stretched out across the inhospitable landscape of Zorandor VII. It was encircled by a desert region, where temperatures ranged from sweltering heat to a frozen waste land. The climate of Zorandor VII was so unpredictable that few people ventured out of the larger towns and cities, as it was more than possible that you could fall victim to the incredible heat, or freeze to death in a storm of snow and ice.

Zol was a labyrinth of streets, many of which looked the same, but in the centre of the city, the financial institutions, lawyers' offices and large business enterprises co-existed. The tall, sleek buildings dominated the skyline of the inner city.

In the daytime the area was a hub of activity, with people and hover-cars hurrying here and there, and fast-food outlets of all kinds doing a roaring trade, catering for the busy workforce and business clients. But at night, in the cover of darkness, the city had a sinister edge. Most of the lights in the offices were out, and a cool breeze blew down the narrow streets.

Gilbert's office was on the sixth floor of a tall office block, and was one of the few with the lights still on. He often worked late, which was the main reason for his history of failed relationships, and almost non-existent social life.

On the street below, a shadow emerged from behind one of the closed café bars, and eased its way along the edge of the office building. There were no guards, as there was nothing to steal. All company information was held on the central web, and in any case, electronic eyes surveyed almost every corner of the inner city – almost every corner …

The shadow neatly dodged all of these devices and began to Ghost into the main office complex …

Gilbert shuffled the papers on his desk, checked his watch, and sighed deeply. It had been a long day, and the case had become troublesome. He had a good idea of what was happening, and it worried him immensely. As for the Group agent they had been looking for – if Meloney couldn't find him he must be good, and now, another dead end.

Gilbert washed his hands in the basin next to his desk, and with a weary sigh, reached for his overcoat. He lived only a few blocks away, and always walked home. He glanced out of the window, and heard the familiar sound of police sirens in the distance, not unusual in a city where every manner of crime was committed daily.

He heard a sudden click behind him, and knew instinctively what it was. A bulb flickered as a silhouette was momentarily framed in the doorway, and Gilbert lunged for the drawer of his desk to reach for the gun that he always kept there, but he was too slow …

The long day and uncertain night had taken its toll on Meloney. Removing only her jacket and shoes, she lay back on the hotel bed, fell into an uneasy sleep, and dreamed …

On the ship, they were gaining on her … how had they found her so quickly? What was she going to do? Panic gripped her, but she had to think fast – she was the captain – it was her responsibility.

On the view screen the Group battlecruiser was almost upon them, and a message was being sent repeatedly:

"You will surrender your vessel immediately or be destroyed – prepare to be boarded." Meloney and her crew had rescued a colony

of slave workers from the planet Zar, and were taking them to safety somewhere in the decentralized zone, but Meloney's ship could not outrun or fight a Group battlecruiser.

What about the children? The thought of them going back into slavery on that dreadful colony was too much for her to contemplate – she looked up and saw their parents' pleading eyes upon her – desperate for an answer.

"Prepare to be boarded." They were in the airlock now – not long before they reached engineering, and then ... the ship would be lost – so easy for the Group soldiers to close down the engines and reach the bridge.

She looked at the children huddled together in their parents' grip – terrified.

The Group soldiers had nearly reached the last section of the airlock – twelve of her own crew were in there, waiting to face them – fuse guns against auto-rifles, amateurs against elite soldiers – it would be a massacre. And then ... the children, slavery, or worse, falling into the Groups' 'scientific research' clutches ... the pain probes, the biological and neuro servitors ... the red-coated 'lab explorers.'

Meloney rose from the captain's chair and half stumbled to the electronic control panel. It was locked out by voice command, but Meloney whispered the captain's emergency sequence, nearly getting it wrong in her haste and anxiety.

Her hand trembled over the airlock controls ... how could she justify ...?

One of the children started to sob, her mother cradled the girl, and stared up at Meloney, her eyes full of tears. Another child, a boy, buried his face in the folds of his mother's dress, his body shaking uncontrollably. The mother opened her mouth but no sound came out, only the inaudible scream in her eyes that pierced Meloney beyond all words.

Meloney crashed her hand down on the airlock controls ...

A huge explosion ruptured the airlock between the two ships, blasting the entire section into space, and sending the Group ship spinning away into the void, along with the Group soldiers that were in the airlock ... and half of her own crew.

From the bridge came a terrible wailing, echoing out into the lonely darkness of space, but the wailing was not from the children, shivering in the unreal silence ... but from Meloney, as she slumped to the floor and hid her face from the universe ...

Meloney gasped in her sleep, her body writhing in sweat ... then silence, as she regained consciousness and lay there, unable to move. A new dawn was creeping through her window, and her communicator was beeping rapidly.

Part 2: Evidence

Meloney surveyed Gilbert's office. There was no sign of a struggle, no sign of any violence, and no blood on the carpet. She checked the windows – no sign of forced entry, besides, this high up, it was unlikely ...

Detective Fisher was in charge of the case. He looked Meloney up and down, and watched her search the office.

"It's no good, you know – you won't find anything. We've had the lab people in, they found nothing ..."

"And where was his body?"

"Slumped over the desk, with the gun still in his hand – a clear case of suicide."

"Can I see him?"

"No, his body is in the county morgue, soon to be incinerated. There was a laser wound to the temple – that's all."

"Very convenient," said Meloney. "And what about the weapon?"

"The wound was from a standard laser pistol, nothing special. I expect you're carrying one now – somewhere. And Detective Fisher looked all over Meloney again.

"So why would he take his own life?" Meloney asked, quietly.

"Well, it could be any number of reasons," he shrugged. "Stress, money problems, or maybe …"

"Maybe, Detective Fisher, he was getting too close to something."

"Are you suggesting this was not suicide, Meloney?"

"That's exactly what I'm suggesting, but of course, I wouldn't expect you to go along with that."

"Look," said Detective Fisher, "he had a bad day, he was upset, maybe had a few drinks – we get this all the time. You, private investigators, have too much imagination – a few weeks in the real force and you'd know how common this shit is."

"Well," Meloney replied, angrily, "thanks for caring so much! Any chance of seeing an autopsy or med report?"

Detective Fisher shook his head. "There won't be an autopsy, and the med reports are classified. Anyway, it was clear what killed him."

Meloney turned to him, infuriated. "The only thing that's clear to me is that somebody doesn't want us to know what happened – and that you aren't going to go out of your way to find out!"

Detective Fisher sighed. "I'd advise you to let it go, Meloney, I'd hate to see you get hurt."

"Let it go? He was a man I worked with for ten years – he was my friend, damn it!"

"You'd be better off staying clear of this, Meloney."

"Are you threatening me, Detective Fisher?"

"No, Meloney, this is not a threat – it's a certainty."

Meloney glared at him for several long moments, and then stormed out of the office, slamming the door behind her.

From the window, Detective Fisher watched her cross the street below. "Hmm, such a waste of a pretty girl," he whispered to himself, and then he shrugged again, and sat down, suddenly feeling very tired. He tapped on his communicator. "All done here, sir – nothing to report."

Meloney met Ozzur in a bar near the river, on the other side of the city. Ozzur was from one of the Ghost Moons, and had been a kind of partner/friend to Meloney for a long time. Being from a Ghost world meant that he could disappear in a crowd, or take on a different form for a limited amount of time. But now he was in his more usual humanoid form, tall and thin, but otherwise not noticeably different from the average human.

"Try not to get too upset, Meloney," he said, in his soft, low voice. "I know you worked with him for a long time."

"He didn't kill himself, Ozz – I know it."

"But there was no sign of struggle – you said."

"The cops could easily have tidied the place up before I got there. Also, Gilbert never carried a weapon, especially not a laser pistol – he hated them. All he had was an old service revolver which he kept in his desk drawer, but I noticed the drawer had been locked – and Gilbert always left it open. No, Ozz, Fisher was lying through his teeth – but why?"

"Well, it's impossible to prove one way or another, we have no evidence, Meloney."

"Yeah, I know – the bastards are up to something, Ozz, I can feel it. Gilbert had me tracking somebody – maybe a Group agent. I think

Gilbert had stumbled onto something to do with the Group – and he was taken out."

"If this is true, Meloney, you must be careful – you could be next on their list."

"What am I going to do, Ozz? I know the bastards killed him."

"What about Gilbert's apartment? Maybe we could find something there?"

"No, Ozz, it's too dangerous. The place is bound to be under surveillance, and Gilbert always kept his important papers in the office. Besides, the cops would have removed any evidence by now."

"You look tired, Meloney, go home and rest. Meanwhile I'll do some digging."

"Thanks, Ozz, I appreciate that – but be careful – I don't like the way this is turning."

✷

Meloney could have ordered a hover-car to take her back to her hotel, but instead decided to walk. She needed to clear her mind after speaking to Detective Fisher – there was so much that didn't fit with Gilbert's death, but like a jigsaw puzzle, the pieces needed to be put in place.

Her walk took her through a market district, where various vendors had their stools set out, selling everything from old used library books, to modern gadgets that Meloney couldn't even identify. There was clothing from all corners of the planetary systems, jewellery and gemstones of dubious quality and origin, and various foodstuffs, some of which still looked alive …

She stopped at a few of the stools and made some minor purchases, and then, realising she was loitering aimlessly, resumed her walk through the market towards her hotel.

As she left the market district there was a narrow dirt road that led towards the city, and it was on this road that she recoiled in revulsion at the sinister figure moving towards her. She recognised the wagon and the worn out pony slowly pulling it along, but it was the sight of the old merchant, sitting on the wagon with a vicious-looking whip wrapped around his neck – that always terrified her.

The merchant was like an apparition from one of the ancient horror movies she had seen. His clothing was in tatters, frayed and dirty, with stains on his long sleeves and hood. His sandals were caked in grime, and there was an overall dustiness about him. It was as though he had been buried alive and then pulled up out of the ground. His long, grey straggling hair was filthy, his eyes bloodshot and rheumy, and when he spoke his breath was putrid, his remaining teeth rotten and broken.

When he saw Meloney he halted the cart and leaned towards her. His voice was rusty and whispering dry.

"Ah, Meloney, how nice to see you again."

Meloney felt a shiver run down her spine, she didn't recall ever telling the merchant her name. "I see you've been making a few purchases," he looked at her quizzically. "Anything interesting?"

Meloney fought her revulsion and replied as politely as she could. "No, nothing in particular, bits and bobs."

"Bits and bobs and chimney pots, that's what we all are made of!" The old merchant laughed chillingly, as he half sung the rhyme in a horridly coarse voice.

For the first time, Meloney noticed that his cart was completely empty. No sacks of food, no garments, boxes or barrels had been loaded on the back, as was usual with other merchants and pedlars trading in the markets.

"What is it you are selling?" Meloney asked, her curiosity getting the better of her.

The merchant grinned hideously. "Anything you could possibly dream of, my dear," he answered, lingering on each word, which somehow made it sound slimy and repulsive.

Meloney shuddered, and wished she hadn't asked, but the merchant continued. "I would love to stop and talk to you for eternity, young Meloney, but I must be moving along. Before I go, I have something for you – free of charge."

"Oh, no, really – don't trouble yourself. I'm ... in a bit of a hurry, and ..."

"It's no trouble, Meloney, no trouble at all." The merchant turned around and rummaged in the cart. "Yes, yes, here we are," and he handed Meloney a small silver box. "Don't open it now, or the magic will fly away." He leaned forward again, and spoke very softly. "There is danger on every road, but if you wear this, it will protect you." A ghastly smile spread over his face, and then he turned away. "Gee up, old boy, gee up!"

Meloney let out a sigh of relief as she watched the cart move off towards the market. She looked down at the silver box, and wondered. Somehow it seemed familiar to her. She tucked it into her jacket pocket, and soon she'd forgotten all about it.

She looked towards the market again, but there was no sign of the merchant's wagon – it was as though it had just disappeared into nothing.

The heat of the sun seemed to have left the place, and only rainclouds and darkness remained.

... commence broadcast ...

Group Announcement:

IT IS WITH GRAVE CONCERN THAT THE INTERPLANETARY
GROUP HAS TO REPORT THE STRANGE AND SUDDEN
DISAPPEARANCE OF DR. REGINALD SPOILER, A LEADER IN
THE FIELD OF INDUSTRIAL RESEARCH, AND ONE OF THE MOST
RESPECTED SCIENTISTS OF OUR TIME. IT IS WITH SURPRISE AND
DISAPPOINTMENT THAT THE INTERPLANETARY GROUP NOTED
THE SLANDEROUS AND COMPLETELY FALSE RUMOURS THAT DR.
SPOILER WAS IN SOME WAY INVOLVED WITH THE DISSENTERS,
WHO CONTINUE THEIR MISGUIDED AND DISLOYAL OPPOSITION
TO OUR LAW-ABIDING AND PEACEFUL GOVERNMENT. WE
OFFICIALLY STATE THAT ANY SUCH RUMOURS ARE MERE
HEARSAY AND COMPLETELY UNSUBSTANTIATED. YOU, OUR
GOOD CITIZENS, MAY REST ASSURED THAT THE INTERGALACTIC
GROUP ARE DOING ALL THAT IS POSSIBLE TO LOCATE DR.
SPOILER, AND THAT HE WILL BE RETURNED TO HIS FAMILY IN
THE FORESEEABLE FUTURE. HAVE A GOOD DAY.

... end broadcast ...

Meloney woke from a fevered nightmare, her body convulsing.
But now she lay completely still, like a dead thing. She had seen their
faces, her old crew, smiling at her, telling her she had done the right
thing, to save the others – the children – from slavery. They were
calling out to her, to forgive her, to say it was okay. But she saw their
bodies, blown apart, drifting in space, dying as the airlock was blasted
apart. She climbed back into full consciousness, wiping the tears from
her cheeks as she made herself a strong coffee. She knew the dreams
were a just punishment for what she had done, and she also knew that

every one of her crew would have died for her, died for the children. She knew they would.

She just didn't want them to.

✳

Ozzur appeared in the laboratory on the stroke of midnight. He had calculated this to be the best time to arrive, as only a handful of scientists would be working at this hour, and none of them in this area. The security officers were not an obstacle, as he could easily Ghost past them without being noticed by human or electronic devices. The laboratory was, in fact, well-guarded from human eyes, but none of this had any effect on Ozzur, as he scanned the interior until he found the cubicles for the bodies due for incineration. He soon located the cubicle holding Gilbert's remains.

He hesitated, but realising he must hurry before he returned to complete humanoid form and be detected, he unfastened the safety clasp on the cubicle and, stealing himself for a shock – looked inside – and gasped out loud.

✳

"No wound?"

"Nothing, I couldn't see a single piece of evidence that he'd been shot."

"The rotten bastards – it was probably a lethal dose of poison."

"They took him, and probably used drugs to make him talk – find out what he knew, and poisoned him. The problem is, we cannot prove anything, Meloney. They have passed it off as another suicide and that's that."

"I know, but I'm so angry! We must be able to do something, Ozz!"

Ozz glanced around the bar of the Wounded Dragon, and then whispered:

"Listen, I have arranged a secret meeting tomorrow with one of the leaders of the Dissenters – perhaps we can find some answers."

Part 3: A Trick of the Light

Meloney and Ozzur followed the stranger through the deserted streets. It was just before dawn, before the majority of people began to stir. They had met the stranger outside an empty, ugly tower block that had long since been scheduled for demolition, and made their way on foot towards the outskirts of the city.

This had once been a thriving and fashionable district, with smart offices, large stores selling luxury items, clean streets, and many expensive houses and flats. But the buildings had long been neglected; doors swung on their hinges, windows were smashed, the street-lights vandalised, and piles of refuse had been left to rot in the streets. The air was stale, and the whole area had a sameness about it, a weariness that depressed Meloney and made her feel shabby and down-hearted.

Finally, they stopped, and the stranger led them down some steps that descended into the basement of a large disused warehouse, which was empty save for a few rusty containers, long obsolete machinery, and some frayed rope that hung from the high ceiling.

"Wait here." The stranger turned and walked away.

After several long minutes, low voices could be heard, and a small group of people emerged from behind the containers. They stood in the shadows, their faces indiscernible and inscrutable.

A young woman walked forward, and stood a few paces from Meloney and Ozzur.

"I am called Clarissa. I hear you may wish to join us, but you will have many questions."

"My first question is simple." There was a harshness in Meloney's voice. "Why did you shoot down the *Hard Lines*? There were innocent people aboard that vessel."

Clarissa gestured towards some sacks stacked on the floor. "Come and sit down."

When they were seated Clarissa sighed, and seemed weary. "There is much going on here that you do not understand. Let me try to explain. To begin with, we did *not* shoot down the *Hard Lines* – we do not have that kind of fire-power. The *Hard Lines* was shot down by one of the Group's own battlecruisers."

"But ... why?"

"Don't you see, Meloney? They blame us for it, and so discredit the Dissenters – turn us into the bad guys, so we don't get any support from the civilian population – meanwhile the Group continues to run slave labour from the outer planets, to mine the toxic ore on Xanzi and to take more 'volunteers' for the war with the Fastillions."

Meloney looked downcast. "But to fire on one of their own vessels ..."

"They've done it before – several times. Losing a few cargo ships and freighters doesn't mean anything to them, and the passengers, well, they are dispensable."

Meloney closed her eyes. "It's hideous," she said, her voice shaking. "But what the hell can we do?"

"We can only hope to hinder them, slow them down, and wait for our opportunities. It is a constant game of cat and mouse with their operatives, and we've had some very close calls. We also have to keep moving – we cannot stay in one place for any length of time, in case we are discovered. We are fairly certain that Gilbert was on to them. He'd found out about the slave trafficking from the outer planets, and the illegal mining operations. We also know that he was murdered by the Group, and that the police investigation was a cover-up from the start. Detective Fisher is on their pay-roll, and there was no official police investigation, because they already knew what had happened. The Dissenters are weak – we have some support, but our ships are shot out of the sky, our people disappear, and we are left with nothing – still, we must fight on against the oppression of the Group. Will you join us, Meloney?"

"It looks like I already have."

✱

At a corner table in the Wounded Dragon, Meloney took a sip from her drink, and kept her voice down:

"Do you trust her, Ozz?"

"Think about it, Meloney – the Group wants to discredit the Dissenters, turn them into the enemy, so what do they do? They shoot down one of their own freighters and blame it on the Dissenters – it's easy for them, and the general public will believe it, or they won't care one way or another."

"The majority of people are suffering from a huge dose of chronic apathy." Meloney replied.

"You sound cynical, Meloney, but I think you are correct. Most people will shrug their shoulders and say it's nothing to do with them, and meanwhile, the Group maintains its grip on the planet, and most of the outer worlds. It is a vicious circle of lies and deceit, and has been going on for decades, but I think the war with the Fastillions is reaching a critical point. I've heard talk of heavy Group defeats, but I can't be sure if it's true, so for now, all we can do is wait."

"It all seems so hopeless, Ozz – I feel like we are just throwing pebbles against a brick wall – we don't have the muscle to take on the entire Group fleet, and this business with Gilbert is just so horrible – you know Ozz, I'm starting to feel really scared."

✱

His footsteps were silent, his Ghostly image almost invisible, as he ascended the corrugated- iron steps at the back of the hotel. The grimy windows were streaked with drizzly rain, and a warm wind blew down the narrow alley, where beggars, tramps and outcasts lay huddled under their thin blankets, completely oblivious to all.

Nobody would venture out on such a stifling, airless night – it was perfect for the assassin.

He had been trained to kill quickly and efficiently, and he had never failed. He took no interest in his victims, it was all the same to him, just another job, and as long as he was well paid he cared for nothing else. He meticulously planned each killing, and left nothing to chance. His employers had never seen his face, nor did they care who he was, as long as he got the job done.

And so, his identity remained a mystery, and his motives a dark secret he could never reveal.

Tonight, he was in a foul mood. He was late, due to unforeseen circumstances, and a hitch in his plans. He tried to control his irritation with the situation, tried to concentrate. He reached the window at the top floor of the hotel. The blinds were drawn and the window was locked, but this was no problem. He hesitated for a moment – an easy job, hardly worthy of his particular talents, but then, he had been handsomely rewarded. A young woman – asleep. He could easily take the time to open the window and enter the room by stealth, but again he felt impatient – he needed to be somewhere else – so, somewhat uncharacteristically, he felt a sudden rush of blood and smashed the window noisily.

The young woman stared up at him in the darkness. She had a laser pistol in her hand, and fired two shots straight at him.

Meloney had not been sleeping well. Her dreams had been so bad that she was almost afraid to fall asleep, afraid to drift off into another nightmare, and since Gilbert's death the fear had become even more real. She slept with a gun beside her, not knowing what to expect, and her mind was continuously wandering. She saw conspiracies everywhere, and trusted nothing she heard or saw.

Suddenly the window smashed violently, and there was a strange presence in the room. She could barely make out the shape of the assassin, but her instincts took over, and without thinking, she had already fired her weapon.

Meloney's eyes widened as the laser beam passed right through the assassin's body, and she realized with horror exactly what he was.

The assassin had momentarily been taken by surprise, but he soon recovered. "Ah, not asleep – and you have spirit, at least – but that will not save you." And he edged menacingly closer to Meloney, who backed up against the far wall.

He slowly moved towards her, relishing her fear and confusion, but before he could utter another word, or move any closer to his victim, something had grabbed him, and was pulling him down. He swung around furiously – only to realise – too late, that he had been taken by surprise by another shadow, another Ghost, much like himself.

His last thought was that at least he would be taken out by one of his own kind.

Meloney sat on the bed, shaking with terror, while Ozz held her close. For a long time neither of them spoke, and then Meloney turned to Ozz. "You saved me – but how did you know …?"

"One Ghost can always find another – and I was looking for him."

Somewhere in the city, two silhouettes were sitting, smoking. The blinking neon signs cast beams of fractured light across the walls of the darkened room. The sounds of the street below could be heard through an open window. The night was humid and the city seemed to be suffocating in the oppressive heat, half comatose, but too exhausted to stir.

It was a high office block, the same as any other, new, bland and nondescript. The low hum of the ceiling-fan persisted, as it whirled continuously, disturbing large stacks of documents which were held down with paper weights, ornaments and ash-trays.

One of the silhouettes shifted in its seat.

"So, the assassin failed – first time for everything."

"And the last," the other silhouette replied, mirthlessly.

"Do we send another?"

The first silhouette was silent for some time, and smoke rings curled in the air.

"We do nothing. It is ceasing to matter now – we have more serious problems."

"Yes, well, I've been hearing things, but which stories to believe ...?"

"The truth is, the war is going badly for us – far worse than is commonly reported. The Fastillions have overrun two more of our satellite planets recently, and our supposedly indestructible fleet has been decimated. Our ships' captains report heavy losses, and morale is at its lowest. Our soldiers have no will to fight – one crew even mutinied! At home we are facing open rebellion – not only from the Dissenters, but also from several voices within the Group. Personally, I can only see this ending one way."

"But the Fastillions ..."

"They have faster and better ships than us, and they are impossible to track – they just seem to appear out of nowhere."

"So, what's our next move?"

"We must try to hold on to our conquered planets for as long as we can, but it is getting more difficult with each defeat – eventually, we may have to surrender to them."

"But that would mean the end of the Group ... the end for us."

The Dream Merchants

"Well, I for one intend to be a long way from here before that happens."

✳

At the bar of the Wounded Dragon, Meloney was on her third, but it was not having the desired effect. The bartender this evening was young Floyd, whom Meloney pitied greatly, as he was constantly being harangued by his older colleague, who was always in a bad mood.

"So, the dragon's still wounded?" Floyd smiled at her as he poured.

"Yeah, I dream of her sometimes." Meloney tried to smile, but it failed to materialize. She was thinking of Gilbert. She was tired, sad and angry, and when she tried to speak, it turned into a choked sob. "It shouldn't have ended like this ... Gilbert ... it wasn't right – and there wasn't a damn thing I could do about it!"

Floyd lowered his voice. "I knew Gilbert. He came here for a beer sometimes. He was a good man." Floyd hesitated, and then continued. "You can only remember him for what he was – what he stood for."

"I know," Meloney replied, "but it's not enough! I'm trying to drink myself numb, but it's not working."

Floyd put the stopper in the bottle. "No more for you, Meloney – why don't you have something to eat instead?"

"Thanks, Floyd, but I'm really not ..."

Suddenly the large screen flashed into life, and the regulars all turned to read the message:

... commence broadcast ...

Group Announcement:

GOOD CITIZENS OF ZORANDOR VII, IT HAS COME TO OUR ATTENTION THAT FALSE REPORTS ARE BEING CIRCULATED REGARDING THE PROGRESS OF OUR MILITARY CAMPAIGNS

AGAINST THE FASTILLIONS. ALL SUCH REPORTS SHOULD BE IGNORED, AS THEY ARE COMPLETELY UNFOUNDED. THE CAMPAIGNS ARE GOING EXACTLY ACCORDING TO OUR PLANS AND STRATEGY. WE BELIEVE THESE MALICIOUS REPORTS ARE BEING CIRCULATED BY THE DISSENTERS IN ORDER TO UNDERMINE OUR AUTHORITY, AND TO CAUSE PANIC THROUGHOUT THE CITIES OF ZORANDOR VII. WE CAN ASSURE YOU, GOOD CITIZENS, THAT THERE IS ABSOLUTELY NO REASON TO PANIC. WE WILL, OF COURSE, KEEP YOU UPDATED AS TO THE PROGRESS OF THE WAR. IN THE MEANTIME, WE ADVISE YOU ALL TO REMAIN CALM, AND TO CONTINUE WITH YOUR WORK AND DUTIES AS USUAL. HAVE A GOOD DAY.

... end broadcast ...

There was a general murmur of voices in the bar, and chairs were shifting. Floyd and Meloney looked at each other:

"This doesn't sound right ..." Floyd stammered.

"No, something's happened, Floyd, something big – I can feel it. I better start to make some enquiries." Meloney rose from her seat, but Ozz was already standing in the doorway, with an excited gleam in his eyes:

"It's begun, Meloney – it's begun!"

Meloney and Ozz sat on a sand dune, watching the tide roll in. Despite the news, Meloney was unusually quiet and pensive.

"So, what happens now, Ozz?"

"I guess that will be up to the Fastillions. They are generally a peaceful race – until they are provoked. It was the Group who tried to take over their planet, after all."

"Then they will treat us harshly."

"I doubt it. They have no interest in Zorandor VII. I don't think they'll wish to take over the planet, just make it safe."

"And the Group – have they surrendered?"

"Well, not formally, but they have suffered a huge defeat that wiped out their entire fleet, their leaders have fled, and their supply of slave labour from the outer planets – that will all cease now."

"What about your world, Ozz, and the other Ghost Moons?"

"I don't think they will be affected at all. They were not belligerent, and my people have no argument with the Fastillions. In any case, we are not without our own defences."

"The agent that Gilbert sent me to find – we never did trace him."

"Hmm, my guess is that he was somehow involved with the Group's slavery operations. Gilbert found out about it, and was starting to put two and two together, when he was silenced. I think Clarissa was right. He's most likely outside the system by now. Most of the Group's operatives have fled."

"Then we'll never find him? I don't feel like I've achieved anything, Ozz, it's all so frustrating!"

Ozz touched Meloney's forehead. "How are the dreams?"

"I still have nightmares."

"I can help you. Take your pain away. The dreams – you would not remember."

"No," Meloney looked into his eyes. "I made the dreams, I'll live with them."

"You suffer for deeds of the past."

"I suffer for friends who will never leave me."

Ozz took her hand, and they sat in silence for a long time, until Meloney stirred.

"You saved my life, Ozz. I never got around to thanking you."

"Well, you saved mine once – I owed you one. If it weren't for that …" he shrugged.

"You rotten pig!" Meloney laughed and punched his arm – and then she felt something in her jacket pocket.

"I forgot all about this, Ozz."

"What is it?"

"A free gift from a scary old merchant – he said it would protect me."

"Show me."

Meloney took the small silver box from her pocket and pulled the lid off. She gasped in surprise – instead of the old piece of junk she was expecting to see, there was a beautiful half-moon crystal pendant inside, which sparkled in the failing light. Meloney slipped it around her neck.

It felt comfortable, as though it belonged.

"You know, Ozz, I think I might wear this, after all."

Sometime later, Ozz turned to Meloney, and said:

"I must be going soon – why don't you come back with me, Meloney? There's no reason for you to stay here now."

"Oh, I don't know, Ozz. I feel like I owe it to Gilbert to stay, at least for a while."

"There's nothing you can do for him now, Meloney – he would have wanted you to be happy."

"Well, let me think about it, Ozz, I'm all confused at the moment."

It was growing darker, and the Ghost Moons of Zorandor VII were scarcely visible beyond the clouds.

"Your planet is a strange world, Ozz."

"We all live in strange worlds, Meloney – the mind is a strange place."

Meloney laughed. "I can't argue with that! Look at the stars, Ozz, they seem to be fading in and out, just like the Ghost Moons."

"Oh, it's just a trick of the light, Meloney."

She smiled and rested her head on his shoulder.

The waters lapped at the shore.

Re-write

'So, here is my story – the one that was stolen from me ...'

My heart sank. My first thought was, "now I've got to change the opening line." But as I read on ...

I read the entire story, comparing it to my draft copy. But this was *my* story, word for word – even the mistakes I hadn't gotten round to correcting!

It was impossible! Even if somebody had somehow stolen my story, there was no way it could have been published so quickly. My draft copy was only a week old – impossible for somebody to steal it, submit it, and get it published in a week! But here it was, printed in a glossy science fiction mag, with a really good illustration to boot, written by some unknown writer I'd never heard of. How could this be?

I tried not to panic – deep breaths. Was I going crazy? Too much time hunched over the keyboard? No, surely, I'm not that far gone? Take it easy, some coffee and a biscuit. Take a break for a while. Too much reading and writing could do this to you. Too many words. They all look the same after a while.

Writing a story is not so difficult. Once you get an idea you just kind of 'go with the flow'. The worse thing is the reviewing and editing. Hours and hours – and hours! You're never happy with it. There's always a scene you think you should add or omit, always a clearer way to express an idea, create an atmosphere, maybe just change a word here and there. Sooner or later you have to 'draw a line under it', as they say. But there's always this nagging feeling that you could have made it just a little better – oh well, enough of this – try to rest.

I didn't do much that evening. I didn't have the energy to go for a walk, and it was raining anyway. So, I stayed in and watched an old black and white movie I'd seen many times before, but it was still pretty good. American gangsters and a washed-up hero who came through in the end. All a bit naff these days, but at least it wasn't dark, brooding and bloody depressing like modern films tend to be.

The next morning I decided to have a day out to clear my mind and so I took a train into London.

It was raining when I stepped out of the underground at South Kensington, but I didn't mind. I purchased a newspaper from one of the kiosks, and after glancing at the lurid headlines, wondered why I had bothered. It was more of the usual – economic disaster, war and politics, 'celebrities' I'd never heard of ... I sighed, and threw it in a wastepaper bin.

I was feeling hungry by then, so I searched the streets for a while and found a 'greasy spoon' café that wasn't too greasy. I chatted with an old couple about the awful state of the weather, and when they left, I gazed out of the café window for some time, watching the people passing by. The great tapestry of life was never complete, and the Fates held the slender threads loosely in their hands. I rose from my seat, thanked the waitress, left a tip, and headed towards the museums.

The fine Victorian buildings always impressed me, and as I entered the Natural History Museum I was immediately overawed by the huge skeleton of 'Hope', the enormous blue whale, suspended from the ceiling in the beautiful entrance-hall. The last time I had visited the museum, there was the gigantic 'dippy' the diplodocus on display, which was equally impressive, but the blue whale somehow felt a lot more immediate, part of our 'real world', and I stopped in my tracks to admire this wonderful creature that mankind had so nearly hunted to extinction.

I began to have a look around, and spent some time examining the fossils, minerals, plants and insects on display in various glass cabinets. It was humbling to think that all of these life-forms had been on the planet so much longer than mankind.

I carried a small notebook with me, and jotted down a few words, maybe for a new story, or just to inspire some ideas. The truth was, that after my earlier shock, I was trying to relax, and get away from my tiny flat for a while.

I had to visit the dinosaur gallery now that I was here, so after grabbing a quick coffee in the café, I made my way there, not really knowing what to expect.

The huge presence of the T-Rex daunted me.

How terrifying must the *King of the tyrant-lizards* have been in real life? I imagined the huge creature tracking me stealthily through a dark and misty primordial forest, and I shuddered when I looked up at those serrated teeth, and cold remorseless eyes – this monster was a killer – pure and simple. Like a Great White shark, all it did was exist, hunt and feed – a bloody scary concept.

I left the museum around 4pm and it was already getting dark. I purchased an over-priced sandwich at the station and began the long journey home, with some nice postcards from the gift-shop, a half-moon shaped 'fossil', that for some reason I felt compelled to buy, and a notebook full of scribbled hieroglyphics.

It was late by the time I got indoors, and I was very tired, so I went to bed, and lay awake for some time, before I finally drifted off into a very strange dream.

I was sitting on a far-away beach counting the waves as they crashed upon the rocks and broke upon the shore.

But I grew weary, and, after concentrating for a long time, I found that I had lost count of the waves. I grew embittered and cursed at the sea for wasting so much of my time.

At that moment a white fox appeared out of nowhere and asked me:

"Foolish man, why do you spend your time worthlessly counting the waves, and idling your life away?"

I had no answer for the fox, so I just shook my head and said nothing.

"Forget the waves that have passed," said the fox, "count only those that are still ahead of you."

And the fox disappeared.

I woke from my dream, knowing that I'd heard this story before somewhere, but I couldn't quite place it. I took my time getting dressed and boiling the kettle. I rubbed the side of my face and decided I needed a shave, so I clumped up the stairs into the bathroom. I started to think of my story again. It couldn't be right – surely, I must have been seeing things?

When I looked in the mirror I saw a face I knew, but didn't know. It was my face, but much older. The lines were more prominent, the eyes a little sunken, and the hair was greying.

I was about to speak when the reflection spoke to me.

"I am your older self. I am here to give you some sound advice."

"What advice?" I was shocked and thought this must be some weird daydream or illusion.

"Stop writing. Try doing something else."

"But my story ..."

"It is average at best. Nobody will be interested. It will not affect your life."

I felt insulted. No writer likes to be told their story is 'average at best'.

"How do you know anything about my life?"

"*Because I am you!* I've been striving for years to write a great story. Okay, I've had a few published, but none of them have brought me any great success – you're wasting your time."

"And how do you measure success?"

"Well, it's not *all* about money, but it helps!"

"No, no – that's not it at all! I don't *care* about the money. That's not why I write."

"Well then, what's the use …?"

"Somebody once said that an untold story is a crime – or words to that effect. I write stories because they are important. They define us. Without our stories we are nothing."

"Well, that's one point of view, but it doesn't pay the bills."

I was now very curious. "So, why are you trying so hard to put me off?"

"I just think you should do something a little more … lucrative … with your time."

I became angry. "Well, that's up to me, isn't it – and you only know *your* story, not mine."

"Suit yourself. You always were a stubborn bastard. But don't forget I tried my best to warn you."

I was hurt and upset, and turned away from the mirror. How should I respond? Should I take his advice? I looked back at the mirror defiantly, and saw my own 'real' face staring back at me – the apparition had gone.

I calmed myself and sat down, then I remembered. "Hey, I thought he said he had some stories published – that's not so bad." I went back downstairs and picked up the mag where 'my' story had been printed. It wasn't there. Instead there was a different story, by a different writer.

For the first time I thought of using a pseudonym. "Yeah," I said to myself. "My real name is not so great. A pseudonym would be better. What name was I thinking of? No matter, I'll remember it later. Now, let's get on with it." I hunched back over the keyboard and began to type, and type, and type.

At some point I fell asleep, and woke just before dawn. Thankfully, there were no more dreams, but I felt cold, and wrapped my dressing-gown around me. I needed a hot drink to get myself going again. In a half-conscious daze I tottered towards the kettle, and while I waited for the water to boil, I read the first line of my new story, and this time I knew it was good.

'So, here is my story – the one that was stolen from me …'

Volume 2

Drabbles
(100-word fictions & sketches)

Monsters!

Nobody believes your silly tales.

They say you're a strange child, who makes up weird stories and lies.

When they found the bodies with their heads twisted off and fur ripped out they said you had 'anger issues' and needed help, tearing up your toys like that.

But they haven't seen the monsters – with their nasty little smiles at night, just waiting for you to fall asleep.

You can feel them all around, as you lie awake, watching their shadows crawl across the ceiling and walls.

Every night they creep closer and closer – until – but nobody believes your silly tales.

Wolf at the Door

Mr. Wolf sat up in bed and wondered why he felt uneasy.

Rain was beating against the rattling windows.

He heard a footstep on the stairs, and knew that something dreadful was about to happen.

He took off his glasses, put down his book, and doused his cigarette in the empty beer can.

A light tap on the door – a loud clap of thunder, and his voice shivered, "Come in."

The moon went out.

Darkness entered the room.

His fur stood on end.

And the last thing he saw as the lightning struck –

the cruel crimson hood – descending on him …

The Second Sack

Santa slung two sacks over his shoulder and called for his reindeer.

The first sack was bulging with the gifts of love.

The second sack was empty.

When the long night was over, and all the gifts were delivered, Santa returned to his winter home high in the mountains, and quietly locking the door, untied the second sack, which was now full to overflowing.

Slowly and reluctantly he picked out the top letter, opened it, and began to read silently.

Sometime later, the reindeer heard a familiar muffled sound, and lowered their heads.

It was the sound of Santa weeping.

Not the Removals Game

"Sweat's running down me back – that one was bloody heavy!

They don't even need any of this stuff, but they insist on taking it. Flaming cart's busted too, and me boots need mending.

Feels like I've been doing this for ever! Shifting souls up & down, up & down – me and me mate are knackered!

The boss down there – he tells me to stop complaining. The boss up there – he tells me the same!

But when do I get a rest? I keep asking, but they don't answer.

Oh, blimey! Not another one.

"'Hello mate – you for up or down?'"

The Sage

The sage took five students into the mountains and left them there.

On arriving home he felt sickly, and the village elders grew concerned: "Which of your students is the worthiest? Which one will succeed you?"

The sage was silent.

After three days two of his students returned.

After seven days two more returned.

"Where is the last disciple?" the sage asked, his voice very frail.

"Nobody knows," the elders replied. "He wandered off into the mountains."

"When he returns," said the sage, "he will be my successor."

And with these words, the old man died, and the village mourned.

Respectable

Two respectable old gents sit at the table in the bar. They keep their voices down.

"Just one more job?"

"This one's a doddle!"

"There's only two guards – probably be asleep."

"The windows are never bolted."

"The doors are never locked."

"The cameras – switched off."

"The alarm – disconnected."

They take another swig of beer.

"We'll be in and out in no time."

"No one will know until it's over."

"Done and dusted!"

They sit back and relax. Five pints later they lean over the table and leer at each other.

"So, one more job?"

"How about just one more pint?"

Wishes

"Where did you find it?"

"Outside the gates, sir."

"Did you see who left it?"

"No, sir."

"Go." The slave fled. The genie struggled from the bottle, looking confused.

"Who summoned me?" he stammered. "Oh ... you're still entitled to three wishes ... it's the rules."

"I forego the first two wishes."

"And the third wish?" The genie's voice trembled.

"I wish there were another way." And the genie was sealed back in the bottle, and cast into eternal flames.

The fallen angels looked perplexed, but Lucifer just smiled sadly and shook his head. "No wishes are granted in Hell," he whispered.

Killer

Inspector Harvey threw his hat on the bar and sighed.

"Another one – right under our noses!"

This was victim number five, all young women, all beaten and strangled in the night. Lou, the barman, kept quiet. He knew this was a bad one.

It was firework night. Every available officer had been patrolling the area. Inspector Harvey had paused on the bridge to watch some of the display.

At that very moment, the killer had struck again. Lou leaned over and whispered:

"Inspector, why does he do it?" Harvey picked up his hat.

"I wonder ... if he even knows himself."

Whitechapel, 1888

How many pipes now?

It doesn't matter.

The opium fills his head with lurid dreams. Dreams and nightmares, remembrances of all that might have been.

His regrets are ashes.

A haze of smog smothers London, as in the night a woman screams and dies.

Top hats and canes tap the veins of the streets. The lascar grins at his profits.

How many pipes now? It doesn't matter.

He is only another lost in the fog.

In the morning, he lays on his cot, and can no longer hear the hansom cabs rushing by, uncaring.

How many pipes now? It doesn't matter.

Mona Lisa Blues

Every night, she watches the cars go by, until she can't tell them apart – their bleary headlights in the rain, the neon signs above the drug stores and cafes.

The demons from the past.

She sways to the beat from the club in town, and when she's sad, the music soothes, and sends her off to sleep, until the light of dawn wakes her anew.

And sometimes she looks out, and sees a rainbow in the sky, and slipping on a summer dress, she steps into the night – with the Mona Lisa blues, and a mystery in her enigmatic smile.

Seasons

Winter: Outside the church, Bob leans on his crutches and reaches into a bag. His hands shake with cold as he breaks bread with the pigeons.

Spring: From the classroom window, Miss Clark watches the children skipping and playing. The years passed like shadows, just memories now.

She turns away slowly, wiping her eyes.

Summer: Eddie, sweating, runs the traffic lights. They're getting too close! His heart nearly stops at the shriek of a siren.

Autumn: Jenny picks at the clothes in the outdoor market. She's young and so pretty, but when she smiles you know her heart is broken.

Butterfly

(after Chuang Tzu 369-286 BC)

The girl ran across the sunlit fields, holding her net aloft to catch the butterfly, but she grew weary in the summer heat, and yawning, she stretched out on the grass.

She lay there, hearing only the wild birds' call, and the calm lapping waters of the glassy lake.

And soon she began to dream.

She dreamed she was the butterfly, with the whole freedom of the sky – and a young girl, running, with net held high.

And when she woke, she was no longer sure if she was the girl chasing the butterfly, or the butterfly, trying to escape.

Drizzle

Happy old Harry leans on his stick and stands outside the local bookies.

It starts to rain in a fine drizzle.

"Bastard horse," he mutters under his breath. "Bastard."

His wide-brimmed hat keeps the worst of the rain off as he shuffles wearily to the bus-shelter, where a young woman with a child in a push-chair brushes past him.

Harry looks away. "Bastard rain," he whispers.

He traces the outline of the hip-flask in his coat pocket, but leaves it where it is.

Twenty minutes later he looks bitterly down the long stretch of deserted road.

"Bastard bus," he mumbles.

Odds

Grumpy old Joe sits in the café with the sports pages open.

Muttering to himself, he sips his tea and scrutinizes his betting-slip. This one's a winner – he can feel it in his bones.

He fumbles for some coins in his patchwork pockets, and counts them out on the table-cloth.

Through the frost in the windows, he watches the people rush by.

The young waitress hovers.

"Look at them," he snarls. "Always in a bloody hurry."

"It's very cold out there."

"It's a lot colder in here!"

She frowns, and scurries off behind the counter.

He re-calculates the odds.

Paradise

"So, Lord, lead me to your Paradise, for I am weary, and my time has come."

"Err, not so fast." The little demon poked his head out from behind a pew. "There's just one more thing ..."

Five years passed, and the old priest knelt before the altar...

"Err, not so fast – we're not quite done yet."

Another five years passed, and the priest was filled with sin, but still, he knelt ...

"Err, not so fast, there's this last little job ..."

Ten years passed, and the demon looked nervous as the priest turned to him:

"You! I haven't finished with you!"

Lost

"So, where is it?"

"I don't know. I haven't touched it."

"Who else could have picked it up?"

"All I know is, I put it here earlier, and now it's gone."

"So, you accuse me of taking it!"

"There hasn't been anybody else here, has there?"

"You must have left it somewhere else."

"It's not somewhere else! I know where I left it!"

"Well, maybe the Fairies took it when you weren't looking!"

"Maybe they did!"

"Don't be a fool – there's no such thing as Fairies!"

"Where the hell is it, then?"

And Then There Were …

Captain Henson was tired, scared, and out of ideas.

"How many left now?" he whispered to Tolby, the ship's doctor.

"Only five of us, captain."

"Edmunds?"

"No, sir."

"Damn it all! What's happening? Who's doing this to us?"

For the last twelve days the crew, originally twenty-five men and women, had been vanishing without trace in this strange, uncharted star system.

The ship's distress signal called out across the empty void: *This is the Earth exploration vessel Medusa … please respond …*

By the thirteenth day, the corridors were silent. There was no life aboard.

Alone, the *Medusa* drifted in deep space.

Trick or Treat?

Tom grinned. "What a great Halloween!"

"Yeah, must be the costumes."

The costumes *were* cool. Tom had the Dracula cape and mask – crazed red eyes and dripping fangs, and Jim was Frankenstein, with a glistening bolt through his neck.

Jim hesitated. "It's getting late. The last house is Mr. Elkin's place, near the woods, but ..."

"Oh, well, if you're *too scared*, I'll go instead."

Jim ran off, but when he returned, he was shaking as he held out a strange old coin. "He gave me this."

"But Jim, the house is empty. Mr. Elkins died ... thirty years ago."

Firework Night

"Wow! See that rocket!"

Tom's eyes were shining.

The two boys shivered in the cold, despite their coats, hats, and gloves.

The explosions thrilled them and scared them. The night was aflame with colour, noise, and wonderful patterns of light, as fireworks danced, dazzled, and expired.

Jim pointed. "Look."

This one hadn't expired, but kept going, higher and higher, until it was out of sight in the dark November sky.

Jim whispered. "I'm not sure that *was* a firework."

"What do you mean?"

"I think it might have been ..."

They glanced at each other, and a secret was shared forever.

In the Enemy Camp

I wake to the sound of soft rain falling and the murmuring of low voices.

I can hardly believe it – I've survived the attack and seen another dawn! My body is a desert of pain, my mouth dry, my eyes half-blind.

I cough and it hurts. I have no voice.

I don't know if we've won or lost the battle.

Two warriors and a beautiful shield-maiden enter the tent and stand over me. I don't recognise them, but they wear the dark colours of our enemy.

"Good," says the maiden. "He is still alive. Now we can kill him properly."

Viking

The arrow in his chest is deep, but he feels no pain.

He has killed three men in battle, and will die content, with a sword in his hand.

The raid has been a great success.

Through dimming eyes he glimpses their dragon ship, ready to sail. Against the sunset, she looks glorious.

His friend kneels beside him, and tries to remove the arrow.

"No, leave it." He slowly pulls off an arm ring. "For my wife. You won't forget?"

"I won't forget."

He sees the great hall of Valhalla, and the beautiful Valkyries beckoning.

And then he is gone.

Almost

She is safely through the first checkpoint.

They pass her documents between them, endlessly scrutinizing the details. It is snowing hard, and biting cold. Visibility is poor, and through the binoculars, it is hard to see properly.

The woman stops by the barbed wire fence, waiting for the barrier to be raised. Spotlights follow her in the dark.

They wave her through the second checkpoint.

Two sentries open fire at the same moment – and the woman falls to her knees and dies in the snow.

Agent Spender takes his hat from the broken hat-stand.

"Bloody shame – she almost made it."

Resistance

Half way through the third act she slips out of the theatre into the drizzly rain of the Berlin streets.

The American zone is quiet tonight, but a dog snarls a warning somewhere in the dark.

She crosses the square – the old rendezvous point – and sees a ghost in the fog.

Why did she come back?

She stops at a newspaper stand and asks the man for a light. He shields the flame from the wind. "Nice weather," he says, ironically, and sees memories leap in her eyes.

"I've known worse." She turns away and walks off into the night.

Ghost Wind

The blinds are all drawn, and the lights are all out.

An empty can kicks itself down a deserted street, and 'Closed' signs rattle in hollow doorways.

A broken church bell lies half submerged in the dirt, and tall skeletal trees cast long shadows of fear.

Burnt out carriages rot in their sidings, and a pale face in the mirror haunts the station hotel.

And not a voice can be heard.

Only the ghost wind, low and cool, breathing through the dusty town. A town shrouded in perpetual darkness, where the light of the sun was erased from the sky.

Cuckoo

Cuckoo the clown walks slowly towards his trailer, and hesitates.

He looks up at the darkening sky, pats the bottle he is carrying, unlocks the door, and goes inside.

He cleans off his makeup, pulls off his wig, and pours himself a drink.

"Not a bad night, tonight," he whispers. "A decent crowd, laughing at us – with us – who knows? The whole world's a joke if you think about it."

He switches on the radio and leans back on the couch.

An hour later the bottle is empty, and he is asleep, with a sad little smile on his face.

Gold

The shabby old knight rode up to the huge ferocious dragon.

His armour was rusty, his sword was blunt, his shield buckled, his lance busted, and his horse knackered.

"I've come to take your hoard of gold."

"Nice idea," smirked the dragon, "I like your sense of humour – you think you could take me in a fight?"

"Na, not a chance," the knight replied.

"Then why should I give up the gold?"

"Well, there is one thing," and the knight whispered three words in the dragon's ear.

The dragon turned pale (green) – "Holy shit! Take it all – I'm outta here!"

Cobra!

(The Valley of the Kings, 1925)

"They are guardians, sir."

"Guardians? A row of snakes?"

"Cobras – they guard the tombs against intruders – the workers don't like it, sir."

"Listen, they may have believed all this nonsense about gods and the Underworld three thousand years ago, but this is the twentieth-century! Now – get them working!"

But the excavation faltered, and as the sun rose over the great pyramids, a man came running from the tents below. "Quickly, come quickly – it's the master!"

They found him dead, a look of horror in his staring eyes, and deep puncture wounds in his neck – the marks of a cobra's strike.

Grandmaster

I don't like these pieces.

The armies are merging together, confusing me.

And by my elbow, a clock is ticking.

I can't see a move.

I hesitate, and watch the grin on my opponent's facing spreading.

Perhaps I should resign.

But then I remember my father, teaching me how to play, with a worn out chess-set he'd won in a poker game.

For years we played, until I started to win, and then he said it was time for me to stand on my own.

I smile and relax, and suddenly the game is easy.

I push a pawn forward.

Prophecies

Blood-stained and dying, King Arthur closed his eyes. He saw Excalibur, the lake, Avalon, and the veil of time unravelling before him.

"Merlin told me it would be like this," he smiled.

And Merlin dreamed.

This time he saw it all – the red and white dragons, engaged in furious battle, the swords, the canons – and beyond. He saw the soldiers, the tanks, and the bombs …

"This world is destined for war. Always war. Will there ever be peace?"

The shadow gave no answer, but pointed to a set of scales in the distance, precariously balanced.

Merlin weighed his prophecies.

Masterpiece

"This time." Tentatively, he begins to form an image.

It's slow work, laborious, but at last he starts to apply the brush. His mind slips away into a world of colour, texture and light.

Hours go by, but he is oblivious to the passing of time. Finally he stops, and turns up the lamp, looking upon his creation.

After a while, he mumbles and groans.

"No! No! That's not it – I cannot do it!"

And he tears down the picture, shaking and sobbing, until he sinks into an exhausted slumber.

Later, he stands again and faces the canvas.

"This time."

Milton Keynes UK
Ingram Content Group UK Ltd.
UKHW020435221223
434667UK00001B/1